GHOULFRIENDS
forever

ALSO BY
GITTY DANESHVARI

School of Fear

School of Fear: Class Is NOT Dismissed!

School of Fear: The Final Exam

GHOULFRIENDS forever

WRITTEN BY
GITTY DANESHVARI

ILLUSTRATED BY
DARKO DORDEVIC

WWW.ATOMBOOKS.NET

ATOM

First published in the United States in 2012 by Little, Brown and Company
First published in Great Britain in 2012 by Atom

A CIP catalogue record for this book
is available from the British Library.

ISBN 978-0-349001-21-0

Printed and bound in Great Britain by
Clays Ltd, St Ives plc

Papers used by Atom are from well-managed forests
and other responsible sources.

MIX
Paper from
responsible sources
FSC
www.fsc.org   FSC® C104740

Atom
An imprint of
Little, Brown Book Group
100 Victoria Embankment
London EC4Y 0DY

An Hachette UK Company
www.hachette.co.uk

www.atombooks.net

To my favorite madrileñas,
Francesca and Olivia Knoell

CHAPTER one

nestled deep within the lush forests of Oregon was a small and seemingly average town. Much like any other town in America, it had shops, restaurants, small family homes, and, of course, schools. So normal was the appearance of the town that it was actually quite forgettable. Every year countless travelers passed through without giving it so much as a second thought, utterly unaware that there was anything extraordinary or unique about the place. But, of course, had anyone stopped for a closer inspection, it would have become readily apparent that the town of Salem catered to a rather specific clientele—monsters!

And while one might think that a town of monsters was terribly intriguing, it wasn't. Salem had long puttered by with nary a scandal or drama outside of the occasional spat over which cemetery would host the Dance of the Delightfully Dead, a celebration of the happily departed. In fact, so unremarkable was the community that the most exciting thing on the horizon was the start of a new semester at Monster High.

Bright and early Monday morning, the well-worn wrought-iron gates to Monster High creaked open to a fast-approaching blitz of bodies. Amid the throngs of monster students was a petite gray gargoyle outfitted in a delightful pink linen dress with a Scaremès scarf wrapped stylishly around her waist as a belt. Moving carefully through the crowd, the young girl minded her Louis Creton luggage and her pet griffin, Roux, but mostly her own two hands. As gargoyles are crafted of stone, they are burdened with both extreme heaviness and terribly sharp claws. And the last thing she wanted to do was snag her dress on the first day at a new school.

"*Pardonnez-moi*, madame," Rochelle Goyle called out in a charming Scarisian accent as she crested the building's front steps. "I do not wish to impose upon your business, but might you be looking for this?"

Rochelle bent down, picked up a raven-haired head with crimson lips, and handed it to the imposing headless figure standing next to the main doorway.

"Child, thank you! I keep forgetting my head, both figuratively and literally! You see, I was recently struck by lightning, and it's left me with a spot of what the doctor calls muddled mind. But not to worry, it won't last forever," Headmistress Bloodgood said upon remounting her head on her neck. "Now then, do I know you? In my current condition, I find it hard to remember faces or names or, if I am to be honest, almost anything."

"No, madame, you definitely do not know me. I am Rochelle Goyle from Scaris, and I shall be living in the new dormitory on campus."

"I am awfully thrilled that our reputation as the premier monster academy has attracted so many international students. You've come from Scaris, have you? However did you get here? I hope not atop the back of your sweet-faced griffin," Headmistress Bloodgood said while pointing to Rochelle's peppy little pet.

"Paragraph 11.5 of the Gargoyle Code of Ethics advises against sitting atop furniture, never mind pets! We came via Werewolf Hairlines, a most reliable company; the planes even come equipped

4

with reinforced steel seats for those of us made of stone," Rochelle said as she looked down at her slim but weighty figure. "Madame, might I bother you for directions to the dormitory?"

Before Headmistress Bloodgood could respond, however, Rochelle was thrown to the ground by what felt like a wall of water. Hard, damp, and extremely cold, an unknown entity instantly covered both Rochelle and Roux in a dense, misty fog. Looking up from the floor, she saw a short, rotund woman with gray hair storming through the crowd like a tsunami, knocking over everything within a five-foot radius.

"Miss Sue Nami?" Headmistress Bloodgood called out as the watery woman rammed an unsuspecting vampire into a wall.

Upon hearing Headmistress Bloodgood's high-pitched voice, Miss Sue Nami turned and stomped back, leaving a path of puddles in her wake. Up close, Rochelle couldn't help but notice the woman's permanently pruned skin, crisp blue eyes, and unflattering stance. With her legs a foot apart and her hands perched on her shapeless hips, the woman very much reminded Rochelle of a wrestler, albeit a male wrestler.

"Yes, ma'am?" Miss Sue Nami barked in a piercingly loud voice.

"This young lady is one of our new boarders, so would you mind showing her to the dormitory?" Headmistress Bloodgood asked Miss Sue Nami before turning back to Rochelle. "You are in good hands. Miss Sue Nami is the school's new Deputy of Disaster."

Fearing that students might take advantage of her temporary state of absentmindedness, especially where detentions in the dungeon were concerned, the headmistress had recently brought in Miss Sue Nami to handle all disciplinary matters.

"Nonadult entity, grab your bag and your toy and follow me," Miss Sue Nami screeched at Rochelle.

"Roux is not a toy but my pet griffin. I do not wish to mislead you—or anyone else, for that matter. Gargoyles take the truth very seriously."

"Lesson number one: When your mouth moves, you are talking. Lesson number two: When your legs move, you are walking. If you cannot do them simultaneously, then please focus only on the latter," Miss Sue Nami snapped before turning around and marching through the school's colossal front door.

Upon entering the hallowed halls of Monster High, Rochelle was instantly overwhelmed with a serious case of homesickness. Everything around her looked and felt terribly unfamiliar. She was used to lush fabric-covered walls, ornate gold-leafed moldings, and enormous crystal chandeliers. But then again her last school, École de Gargouille, was housed in a chateau that was once the residence of the Count of Scaris. So, as one might expect, Rochelle was rather shocked by Monster High's modern purple-checkered floors, green walls, and pink coffin-shaped lockers. Not to mention the elaborately carved headstone, just inside the main doors, that reminded students it was against school policy to howl, molt fur, bolt limbs, or wake sleeping bats in the hallways.

"*Pardonnez-moi*, Miss Sue Nami, but are there really bats? As I am sure you know, bats can carry a wide variety of illnesses," Rochelle said. Her short gray legs worked overtime to keep up with the stampeding wet woman.

"Monster High employs vaccinated bats as in-house exterminators to eat rogue insects and spiders. With certain members of the student body bringing live insects for lunch, we consider

the bats highly regarded members of the janitorial
staff. If you have a problem with them, I suggest
you take it up with the headmistress. But I *highly*
suggest confirming her head is properly attached
before doing so," Miss Sue Nami grumbled as she

rammed into an open door and, shortly thereafter, a slow-moving zombie.

The stunned zombie teetered sluggishly back and forth before collapsing to the ground, eliciting sympathetic whimpers from both Rochelle and Roux. Miss Sue Nami, however, stomped full speed ahead, totally oblivious to the effects of her reckless marching.

"I do not wish to tell you how to conduct your business, madame. But I must ask—are you aware that you have knocked quite a few monsters to the ground in the short time we have been walking?" Rochelle asked as tactfully as possible.

"That is known as collateral damage in the school-discipline business. Now, stop dawdling and pick up the pace; I'm on a schedule here!" Miss Sue Nami barked. "And if you are capable of both walking and listening, you will enjoy a brief tour along the way. If not, then I am merely reminding myself where everything is! On your immediate right, we have the Absolutely Deranged Scientist Laboratory, which is not to be confused with the Mad and Deranged Scientist Laboratory, currently under construction in the catacombs."

"Isn't that going to be unnecessarily confusing?" Rochelle wondered aloud as she glanced into the room filled with Bunsen burners, vials of colorful liquids, plastic safety goggles, white lab coats, and countless peculiar-looking apparatuses.

"I have decided to disregard your question, as I do not deem it relevant. I will now continue with my tour. The laboratory is currently being used for Mad Science class, in which students produce a wide variety of things, such as lotion for the scaly-skinned, antifungal drops for the pumpkin heads, fur-calming serum for the hairy, organic oil for the robotically inclined, industrial-strength mouthwash for the sea monsters, and much more," Miss Sue Nami explained before stopping to shake her body like a dog after a bath, spraying everyone in a three-foot radius with water. Fortunately, as gargoyles are built to deflect water, both Rochelle and her dress were spared.

"I love water, and even *I* think that was super gross," a scaly-skinned sea creature dressed in flip-flops and well-tailored fluorescent-pink board shorts muttered while she wiped her face with a fishnet scarf.

"Well, at least you don't have a fur 'fro now," a stylishly clad werewolf moaned, touching her long and luscious mane of now wet auburn hair.

"Lagoona Blue, Clawdeen Wolf, do not waste your lives standing around in the hallway complaining. Go and complain in private, like the smart, ambitious monsters you are."

"*Bonjour*," Rochelle mumbled quietly, offering

a painfully awkward smile to Lagoona and Clawdeen.

"A Scaremès scarf as a belt? That's straight out of *Morgue Magazine*! Totally creeperific," Clawdeen complimented her, clearly impressed by Rochelle's chic style.

"*Merci boo-coup*," the gargoyle called out as she jetted after the fast-moving Miss Sue Nami.

"Next we have the bell tower, just behind which you will find the courtyard and the Creepateria, respectively. To your immediate left you have the gym, the Casketball Court, Study Howl, and finally the Creepchen, where Home Ick is taught," Miss Sue Nami said rapidly while storming through the cavernous purple-and-green halls.

After banging into a row of pink coffin-shaped lockers, the puddle-prone woman turned down an adjoining corridor and quickly resumed her tour guide duties.

"Here we have the graveyard, where you can fulfill your Physical Deaducation requirement with Graveyard Dancing, but of course you can also do that by joining the Skulltimate Roller Maze team, which practices next door in the maze. Next we have the dungeon, where detention is held, and finally the Libury, where both Ghoulish Literature and Monstory: The History of Monsters are taught."

"Would it be possible to get a map?" Rochelle inquired politely with Roux perched sweetly on her shoulder. "While I have a most remarkable brain for remembering things, I'm all rocks and pebbles when it comes to directions."

"Maps are for people who are afraid to get lost, or lost people who are afraid to get found, neither of which applies to you. Plus, for the time being all you really need to know is where the Vampitheater is, for the start-of-the-term assembly."

"But I don't know where the Vampitheater is."

"Then I suggest you find out."

"Might you tell me?"

"Absolutely not. We have a schedule to follow, and the Vampitheater is not on the schedule. Now, pick up the pace," Miss Sue Nami yammered as she opened a coffin-shaped door into an adjoining wing of the school.

After walking down a large and somewhat empty corridor, Miss Sue Nami and Rochelle came upon a worn and weathered pink spiral staircase.

"*Pardonnez-moi*, madame, but this staircase does not look very sturdy—or up to date with general safety requirements. Paragraph 1.7 of the Gargoyle Code of Ethics clearly states that I must warn others of danger, so I am warning you now: This staircase is a menace!"

"Stop worrying. You sound like a soggy sock!" Miss Sue Nami barked, quickly quieting Rochelle.

15

While lugging her Louis Creton suitcase up the rose-colored staircase, which groaned mercilessly under her weight, Rochelle felt yet another pang of homesickness. She suddenly missed everything about home, from the Gothic arches of her favorite cathedral to the smooth yet surly manner in which Scarisians spoke. But perhaps most of all—especially while carting her heavy bag—she missed her boyfriend, Garrott DuRoque. He was as handsome as he was romantic. And while they had never sat next to each other on a bench for fear of its collapsing, they shared a great deal more, including a rosebush he had created in her honor.

Upon reaching the top of the stairs, Rochelle was met with a welcome and delightful distraction. Before her hung an intricately woven off-white curtain crafted out of thin, silky strands. Shimmering in the soft light, the material delighted

Rochelle's deep-seated love of fashion and fabrics. She wondered if she would be able to commission a scarf for her *grand-mère*, as Rochelle was sure she too would marvel at the material. The petite gargoyle's gray fingers, adorned with two Gothic fleur-de-lis rings, hovered a mere inch from the fabric. Oh, how she longed to touch the magnificent material, but she didn't dare, for fear that her claws would snag it, as they had so many fine fabrics in the past.

In a flash, Miss Sue Nami thrust her own large, wrinkled hand against the delicate, finely woven shroud, ripping it in two.

"*Quelle horreur!*" Rochelle squealed at the sight of the destroyed material.

"Save your tears; it grows back in seconds," Miss Sue Nami barked as she pointed to a cavalry of spiders frantically weaving above their heads. Twenty quarter-sized black spiders furiously

flung their legs
about in an
arachnid
cancan,
reproducing
the curtain
within moments.
And while Rochelle had never been terribly fond
of the eight-legged creatures, mostly because they
often attempted to take up residency on gargoyles
without asking, she was impressed by this group's
efficient manner of working.

The dormitory was a long and sumptuous
corridor with moss-covered walls and colorful
stained-glass windows that cast bright squares
of light on the silver snakeskin floor. The soft
emerald-colored moss grew unevenly across the
walls, creating a visible topography with peaks
and valleys. Rogue wisps of webbing wrapped

18

around small mounds of greenery hinted at regular spider treks.

"Mr. D'eath, the school's guidance counselor, is currently checking in the boarders," Miss Sue Nami grumbled as she led Rochelle past several doors to a sitting area just off the corridor. "Follow the rules, nonadult entity, and you won't have any problems with me."

"I'm a gargoyle; we love rules. As a matter of fact, we often make up new ones just for fun," Rochelle responded sincerely, to which the watery woman promptly nodded her head and stomped off.

Alone in a new country, with a new language and at a new school, Rochelle had no choice but to summon all the courage she had and confront the situation head-on. And as far as she could tell, there was no better place to start than with Mr. D'eath.

CHAPTER two

Sporting a most miserable expression, Mr. D'eath, a middle-aged skeleton, shuffled into the waiting area. He was the physical and mental embodiment of melancholy, so much so that he could not even recall the last time he had smiled, let alone laughed. Standing with hunched shoulders and a low-hanging head, Mr. D'eath attempted to wrangle the students lingering nearby. However, instead of simply calling to them or even whistling at them, he sighed. And though the sighs began softly, they soon grew quite loud and aggressive. Why, the man was practically wailing before he was able to rally the monsters into a small group around him!

"Hello, students. I hope looking at my bony face and listening to my flat voice does not depress you," Mr. D'eath announced in a monotone manner. "But if it does, I understand."

The glum man then looked at the ground and began sighing again, leaving the students quite bewildered.

"I guess I should tell you which rooms you're in," the man grumbled painfully, as if the mere act of speaking was zapping every last drop of energy he possessed.

Rochelle was instantly mesmerized by the gloomy man, taking his every sigh and frown to heart. A helpful and proactive gargoyle, she found glum and woeful people difficult to be around without giving advice.

"As you can see, there is a ghouls' section and a boys' section. Boys are not to visit ghouls, and ghouls are not to visit boys," Mr. D'eath said as he pointed to a split in the corridor. "Now then, the Chamber of Ghoulery and Foolery has been assigned to Rose and Blanche Van Sangre from Romania."

Tall and sinewy identical twins with raven hair and ashy skin, both dressed in floor-length polka-dot dresses and black velvet capes, pushed to the front of the group.

"Hullo, me name is Rose Van Sangre, and this is me sister Blanche Van Sangre. Ve are gypsy vampires, so ve do not like to sleep in the same place more than three nights," Rose stated coldly in her thick Romanian accent.

"I don't care where you sleep, or even if you sleep. I, for one, haven't had a good night's sleep . . .

ever," Mr. D'eath announced before once again sighing dramatically.

"*Vraies jumelles!* Identical twins! *Gemelli identici!*" a young man hollered abruptly from the back of the group, prompting all to turn.

The unique boy with three heads, whom they would soon come to know as Three-Headed Freddie, had a terrible habit of blurting out his thoughts unexpectedly. And while each of the heads said the exact same thing at the exact same time, all three spoke in different languages— usually Bitealian, Fanglish, and Scarisian; but sometimes Zombese, Goblinese, and Howlish found their way in as well.

"Ve are not identical, and ve do not take kindly to being mistaken for one another, as ve look very different. As any imbecile can see, Rose's hair is *significantly* less shiny than mine," Blanche said angrily before grabbing the large gold key to her room and storming off with her sister.

"The Chamber of Vampires and Campfires will be shared by pumpkin heads Marvin, James, and Sam."

Three petite creatures with noodle-thin limbs and jack-o'-lanterns for heads bounced up to Mr. D'cath, grabbed their golden key, and broke into song.

"*There once was a woman made out of water,*

so mean we told her 'don't have a daughter,'" they sang as their pet bullfrogs chirped loudly, offering the perfect bass accompaniment. It was a rather well-known fact that the amphibians were absolute naturals at maintaining rhythm.

Pumpkin heads, descendants of the Headless Horseman and therefore very distant cousins of Headmistress Bloodgood, often acted as a Greek chorus, singing about nearly everything they saw or heard.

"The Chamber of Fangs and Orangutans is assigned to Three-Headed Freddie alone, as we heard his heads like to talk in their sleep," Mr.

D'eath announced as the boy averted his six eyes in embarrassment.

"The Chamber of Tomb and Gloom is for Cy Clops and Henry Hunchback."

The shy yet handsome Cyclops moved to the side as Henry Hunchback, a ginger-haired boy suffering from extreme curvature of the spine, approached Mr. D'eath for the key.

"Hi, Mr. D., I'm Henry, and I just wanted to say I am super excited to be at Monster High, especially since Coach Igor teaches here. That guy is a legend," Henry said warmly before Mr. D'eath sighed and looked away.

"Everyone loves Coach Igor—the Casketball team, the Fearleading squad, *and* the Skulltimate Roller Maze team. How come no one has such fondness for

the guidance counselor?" Mr. D'eath bemoaned sadly.

"Something must be done," Rochelle quietly muttered to Roux as she lifted the griffin to see the perpetually gloomy Mr. D'eath.

"The Chamber of Voltage and Moltage is assigned to Hoodude, who will not have a roommate, as we were told his shrine to Frankie Stein is rather elaborate."

Hoodude, a human-sized voodoo doll with blue hair, button eyes, and a variety of needles jutting out of his cloth body, was absolutely infatuated with fellow student Frankie Stein. She had, after all, created him in her father's laboratory.

"Thank you, Mr. D'eath," Hoodude said sweetly before puttering down the boys' corridor.

"And finally, in the Chamber of Gore and Lore,

we have Venus McFlytrap, Robecca Steam, and Rochelle Goyle."

While looking around for signs of her roommates, Rochelle's glance landed on an interesting-looking girl with green skin and a half-shaved head. The girl cocked her head to the side and grinned as the vines that coiled around her wrists lightly fluttered their leaves.

Rochelle certainly wasn't in Scaris anymore!

CHAPTER
three

"**g**illary Clinton is my idol," the brightly dressed girl with punk style and elaborate vine bracelets expounded after opening the door to the Chamber of Gore and Lore, with Rochelle trailing behind her. "Did you know she once endured a weeklong hunger strike to protest the dumping of toxic chemicals in the ocean?"

Hanging on the far wall was a portrait of the current International Monster Federation president, Gillary Clinton. As the head of the monster world's governing body, she was heralded by some and demonized by others.

"Fish can easily go without food for a week. Not that it makes Gillary Clinton's act any less commendable. I only mention it because, as a gargoyle, I have a duty to share all pertinent information," Rochelle explained awkwardly before offering her hand to shake. "I'm Rochelle Goyle, by the way."

"The name's Venus McFlytrap, and this is my pet plant, Chewlian," the other girl announced, and flipped her long hot-pink and green striped hair over one shoulder. "I came a little early to settle him into the room. You know plants—they can't stand change,"

Venus continued while rubbing the pink stubble on the shaved side of her head.

"I must say, he has very good dental hygiene," Rochelle commented, looking at the plant's extremely white teeth and bright green gums.

"Yeah, he's pretty spooktacular," Venus said before blowing a pollen kiss—a small puff of orange dust—toward her pet plant.

"*Pardonnez-moi*, this is Roux, my pet griffin."

Roux, wings and tail wagging happily, pranced over to Chewlian to say hello. Unfortunately, as soon as the small gray animal was within an inch of the plant, Chewlian bit her nose. And not just the tip of the nose: The plant managed to get nearly the entire snout.

"No, Chewy!" Venus

scolded. "Sorry about that—he's in a biting stage. His eyesight isn't very good, so he has trouble distinguishing friends from feasts. Is Roux okay?"

Rochelle noted the plant's mischievous and slightly dim-witted grin before checking on the perpetually happy Roux. "Oh yes, she's fine. She's made of granite, so she's rather hard to take a bite out of."

"He really is such a sweetie when you get to know him, but I'd watch your fingers near his leaves," Venus said before glancing around the room. "Look at this place. Do you believe your eyes? I'm horrified!"

Rochelle looked carefully around the small but cozy space, scanning for possible safety violations, but came up empty. Between the finely sanded limestone walls were three pristinely made beds, two medium-sized windows, a wardrobe, and one large, squishy armchair. Much like a sea anemone, the overstuffed piece of furniture looked primed to swallow anything within reach. Covered in mummy gauze and finely woven molted werewolf fur, neither chair nor bedspreads proved horrifying, leaving Rochelle at a loss. "Are you upset they didn't use higher-quality fabrics? You must remember, this is a school, not a five-skull hotel," she explained earnestly.

"Hello? I'm talking about the non-ecofriendly lightbulbs and the lack of a recycling bin. Honestly, this is just plain reckless!" Venus declared as she stomped her pink ankle boot.

Venus McFlytrap was the daughter of the plant monster, and she had inherited a bit of his temper, especially where environmental protection was concerned. And while she tried to control her pollens of persuasion, sometimes it just wasn't possible. Extreme anger or frustration often resulted in pollen-filled sneezes that swayed all in her path to wholeheartedly agree with anything Venus said. Depending on the intensity of the sneeze, the pollen's effect could last anywhere from a few minutes to a few hours. Most egregious, Venus's bright orange pollen was notoriously difficult to get out of clothing.

Just as Rochelle prepared to correct Venus's assessment of the situation as reckless, the door flew open, banging loudly against the limestone wall.

"Heavens to Betsy," a dewy-faced girl covered in rivets and metal plates exclaimed animatedly. "This school is absolutely batty, and I say that in all seriousness, as I just saw a bat in the hallway, but also because it's enormous. I was so lost and frustrated that I started to steam up, making my hair go absolutely bananas. And while bananas may be good for cereal, they're not good for a ghoul's hair!"

The girl, seemingly crafted out of a steam engine, played with her long blue hair while blushing under Rochelle's and Venus's gazes.

"Robecca Steam?" Venus guessed with a smirk.

"Oh dear, it must seem like my brain is rusted! I can't believe I just flung open the door without even mentioning my name! Yes, I am Robecca Steam! Deary me, I haven't been this nervous since I performed my first aerial stunt in front of Father. That was, of course, centuries ago, before I was dismantled; I am absolutely thrilled to be reassembled!" Robecca said as steam exited her ears.

Whenever she was angry or nervous, steam puffed out of Robecca's ears and nose. And while she didn't much care for the vapors, those around her absolutely detested them. Steam outbursts had been known to unpleat many a skirt and to frizz many a monster's

37

fur. However, it must be noted that the steam was not entirely a nuisance, for it resulted in a natural facial—hence Robecca's permanently dewy complexion.

"*Bonjour*, Robecca. I am Rochelle, and I am very pleased to meet you."

"A Scarisian accent! Well, isn't that just the cat's pajamas!"

"Do cats wear pajamas in this country?" Rochelle inquired seriously.

"Dear me!" Robecca roared with laughter. "Wouldn't that be swell? Cats in pajamas!"

The sound of rustling leaves drew Robecca's attention to the pretty green-skinned girl standing next to her.

"Hey, the name's Venus."

"I can't tell you how excited I am to be sharing a room with you guys. This is exactly why I decided to move out of Miss Kindergrubber's house. I knew dorm life would be the absolute bee's knees. Just think of all the fun we're going to have, staying up late talking—"

"I feel I should mention that I adhere to a very strict bedtime," Rochelle interrupted.

"I'm guessing we should probably start getting ready or we'll be late for the assembly," Venus added as she pried a pen from Chewlian's mouth.

"Late! Oh, how I wish that word didn't even exist! You see, I'm a bit hopeless with the time, since my internal clock is off. But I promised myself I'd try harder once I got to school. It's becoming such an awful pain for Penny, my mechanical pet penguin. I'm often so frantic about the time that I leave her places. . . . As a matter of fact, I'm not quite sure where she is right now. I do hope I didn't leave her at the Maul—or, worse, in the bathroom at the Maul. Penny's pretty squeamish about public restrooms. Not that I blame her—

most are desperately in need of a good steam cleaning," Robecca rambled before taking a seat in the armchair and dabbing the residual steam from her forehead.

So earnest was Robecca about her deficiency that her new roommates trusted her to watch the time, quite literally. She was seated directly in front of the clock and told to call out five minutes before they were to leave.

"I think I just spotted the perfect place for my compost pile," Venus gushed while peering out the window.

"Paragraph 1.7 of the Gargoyle Code of Ethics states that it is my duty to inform someone who is in danger. Venus, compost piles are breeding grounds for bacteria. As a matter of fact, scientists believe they're responsible for last year's Rotten Food Flu epidemic in eastern Mongolia."

"You know what else is a breeding ground for

bacteria? Nuclear weapons. So, why don't you focus on those and leave my compost heap alone!" Venus retorted with obvious annoyance.

"Venus, *s'il ghoul plaît*, let me explain. I really do wish you luck with your compost pile. It's just that as a gargoyle, I have a duty to warn those around me of possible danger and to correct those disseminating inaccurate information. Therefore, I would like to point out that nuclear power plants do not breed bacteria. While they can eradicate man- and monsterkind in minutes, they are a highly unlikely source of germs."

"It's ghoul, I get it, you're just trying to help," Venus said genuinely; her temper was both quick to flare and quick to subside.

Rochelle smiled as she joined Venus at the window.

"Look at all these pine trees. Don't you just love fresh oxygen?"

41

"Is there such a thing as *fresh* oxygen? Isn't all oxygen fresh? Although oxygen can be stored in tanks, and I suppose one wouldn't call that fresh," Rochelle pondered quietly.

"You really like to correct people, don't you?" Venus asked with a slight hint of irritation.

"What can I say? I'm a gargoyle," Rochelle replied while absentmindedly tapping a nearby ceramic vase with one of her hard gray fingers. "We very much value accuracy."

Tapping was one of Rochelle's most problematic little idiosyncrasies. While thinking or talking, and occasionally even sleeping, she reflexively tapped her fingers. As one might expect, sturdy surfaces such

as marble, wood, and metal weathered her weighty digits without problem; fragile items such as ceramic vases, however, were not so lucky.

"*Zut!* Boo la la!" Rochelle exclaimed as the vase crumbled into a mess of ceramic shards and water.

"Don't worry about it," Venus responded casually. "There's nothing more depressing than freshly cut flowers; It's like an open casket at a funeral. They might look alive, but they're dead."

Like the onset of the Rotten Food Flu, Robecca's recollection of the time was instant, horrifically uncomfortable, and even a smidge embarrassing.

"How in the name of the flea's sneeze did I do it again?" Robecca hollered with steam exploding from both her ears.

Somehow, while Robecca was anchored in front of the clock, her eyes had wandered down to her rocket boots and she'd begun oiling them, having completely forgotten about the time.

"Remember how I said I would tell you five minutes before we had to leave? Well, that was ten minutes ago!" Robecca babbled frantically. "Come on! There's not a second to waste!"

"Must we run?" Rochelle asked, traipsing sluggishly after Robecca and Venus.

While gargoyles moved with exceptional speed when flying, they were rather slow on their feet. Stone legs simply were not designed for speed; in actuality, they weren't designed for anything other than standing still.

"Deary me, I'm so sorry, ghouls! I really thought I could do it this time. But clearly I was wrong. My tardiness is contagious!" Robecca rambled as she led the way down the pink staircase.

"Seriously, Robecca, it's not a big deal. So we're late for an assembly? Like I always say, don't sweat the small stuff," Venus declared in a terribly West Coast, laid-back manner.

"Is that your way of telling me I look sweaty, or rather steamy? Oh dear! I feel all rusty just thinking about what an awful first impression I'm going to make!"

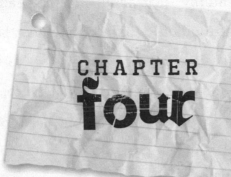

CHAPTER
four

as the eldest and only girl in her parents' garden of monsters, Venus not only was used to being in charge but expected it.

"You guys, stop running! We need to calm down; we're lost in a school, not eastern Siberia. I'm sure if we take a minute to look around, we'll find a map or directory or something to tell us how to get to the Vampitheater," Venus explained rationally.

Frazzled and weary, Robecca and Rochelle nodded their heads before making their way toward an adjoining corridor. Venus, for her part, was momentarily distracted by a headstone warning that the befriending of bats was strictly forbidden because it had been known to breed unbridled jealousy within the local chiropteran community. This phenomenon surprised Venus, as she had always considered bats socially mature, at least in comparison to teenage monsters.

"These big, empty hallways sure do give me the heebie-jeebies," Robecca muttered to Rochelle. "Where is everybody?"

"I'm sorry, but I do not follow. What are the heebie-jeebies?"

"You know, like when the rivets on the back of your neck pop out?" Robecca explained.

"That sounds like being electrocuted, which is a terribly serious matter."

"Guys?" Venus called out, having noted the sudden arrival of a repugnant smell.

In all her years, Venus had never come across such an odious smell—a combination of dampness, pickled cabbage, and day-old liver. So ripe was the scent that she could actually feel fur growing inside her nostrils. And as if the smell were not odd enough, there was now a faint scratching sound, like that of twigs on cement, coming from behind them.

"Robecca? Rochelle?" Venus called out again, louder this time.

Upon hearing their names, the girls immediately turned around, only to gasp, gulp, and groan at what they saw.

49

"What in the name of the foul owl is that?" Robecca shrieked before dramatically covering her mouth with her hand.

"*Quelle horreur!*" Rochelle squealed loudly, her face distorted with revulsion.

A rush of adrenaline filled Venus, spurring every nerve in her body to tingle as she turned to face the great unknown. Standing before her was a morbidly obese troll with leathery skin, infected acne, and long, oily locks covered in mites. As Venus valiantly suppressed the urge to be sick, the lumpy-bodied beast growled and bared his jagged, sludge-covered teeth.

"Think, Venus," she muttered to herself. "What would Dr. Ghoulittle do?"

"Who Dr. Houlittle?" the troll grunted in broken English, masses of spittle spewing from both sides of his mouth.

"Um, he's a ghoul who's really good with

animals," Venus explained awkwardly. "Maybe you've read his books, although I somehow kind of doubt it."

"What you do in hall?" the troll snapped aggressively before again baring his nasty little teeth.

"It's our first day here, and we're lost," Venus explained sensibly.

"Might you be able to direct us to the Vampitheater?" Rochelle interjected nicely.

After a few seconds of intent staring, the troll lifted his hand, showcasing his long and weathered nails, and pointed down the hallway.

"Vampitheater there," the troll barked as a trail of dribble slowly ran across his uneven chin.

"Thanks, you've been really helpful. Well, except for the part where you snarled at me," Venus replied matter-of-factly.

"Next time you late, I eat you," the troll grunted before breaking into a spine-chilling smile.

"Okay, great. That sounds like a plan," Venus said, pulling the other girls away from the troll.

"Am I correct in understanding that he threatened to eat us?" Rochelle asked incredulously.

"Yes, he did, but I wouldn't worry. His mouth didn't look that big. I doubt he could fit more than a hand in it. And lucky for us, we have two of those," Venus replied candidly.

"Heavens to Betsy, being eaten by a troll, or even just nibbled on by one, sounds downright horrendous!" cried Robecca.

"Hey, glad to see I'm not the only one who's late," a well-dressed boy in a plaid cardigan said before holding open the Vampitheater door for the girls.

Venus carefully eyed the boy, amazed by how normal he appeared. Actually, *so* normal-looking was the boy that she couldn't help but think the whole thing was rather *ab*normal!

Venus raised a finger to her lips, quieting Rochelle's and Robecca's murmurs as she led them into the grand purple-and-gold assembly hall. Styled in an Egyptian motif, the large room had statues of pharaohs and sphinxes surrounding the stage. And while Venus was too busy looking for seats to notice the interior, Robecca found the place absolutely magical; she was utterly dazzled by the sparkles and shimmers of the room. Rochelle, on the other hand, found the decor dreadfully tacky and reminiscent of a ride at Grislyland.

After searching futilely for open seats, Venus directed the girls to a pocket of space along one of the auditorium's pathways.

"As you know, gargoyles adore sitting on the ground, since we're less likely to break furniture that way. However, it is my duty to mention that this is a violation of the school's fire code," Rochelle whispered fervently.

"Duly noted," Venus responded as she lowered herself to the ground.

"Isn't this fun? I feel like we're at camp," Robecca said in her sweet yet naive manner.

While cold and hard, the floor actually provided the girls with a fantastic view of the stage. Miss Sue Nami, Mr. D'eath, a gaggle of other teachers they didn't recognize, and a few trolls sat staring at Headmistress Bloodgood as she desperately tried to remember what she wanted to say. Much like steam escaping a boiling kettle, the words had simply evaporated from her mind. More than once she began to speak, only to silence herself seconds later. And then just when she was on the verge of forgetting that she had forgotten anything at all, it came rushing back to her.

"Welcome to Monster High! We are wonderfully frightened to have you here, as this is sure to be our best and most monstrous term yet. There really is nothing quite as exciting as the start of a new semester. For at the beginning you have the opportunity to achieve anything you put your mind to. And as someone whose mind is currently on the fritz due to an unfortunate encounter with lightning, I can tell you what a terrible thing it is to waste," Headmistress Bloodgood said before a bewildered look crossed her face. "What was I saying? Oh yes, of course, the drama department is spectacular here at Monster High. The *Gory Gazette* even called last year's performance of *A Midsummer's Night Scream* 'a real howler'!"

"Ma'am, we were not discussing the drama department," Miss Sue Nami called out. She then approached the headmistress and whispered in her ear, "We are welcoming back the students."

"Thank you, Miss Sue Nami. Your memory of my memory is quite helpful," Headmistress Bloodgood acknowledged sincerely before turning to the audience. "We are absolutely ecstatic to welcome our first class of boarding students to Monster High! As the majority have come to us from faroff places, we converted the east wing's second floor into a dormitory for them! We do hope you like it here, new ones!"

Polite applause filled the Vampitheater as Venus nudged both Rochelle and Robecca. Headmistress Bloodgood was talking about them!

"Now, to introduce another exciting new addition to our school, I would like to call Frankie Stein and Draculaura to the podium."

Two beautiful girls slowly mounted the steps to the stage. Frankie Stein, the daughter of Frankenstein, was hand-sewn, with skin the color of mint chip ice cream, while Draculaura, the daughter of Dracula, was a peppy, pink-haired girl with perfectly sculpted white fangs.

"Hey, everyone, in case you don't know me,

I'm Frankie Stein, and this is my good friend Draculaura. It seems like only yesterday that *I* was the new ghoul at school, trying to find my way around campus. But now look at me! I'm here to introduce another new ghoul—or, rather, the new *teacher*," Frankie said before deferring to Draculaura.

"Please give a warm welcome to Miss Sylphia Flapper, direct from Bitealy, here to teach Dragon Whispering 101," Draculaura said enthusiastically, holding her hands up in the air to applaud.

A beautifully delicate European dragon, closely surrounded by trolls, stepped forward to wave to the audience.

"Oh, and she didn't come alone," Frankie added. "She's brought a team of elderly trolls with her, who, under Miss Sue Nami's guidance, will be pa*troll*ing the halls."

"We trolls! Follow rules!" the oily senior citizens

surrounding Miss Flapper grunted aggressively at the crowd.

"As you can see, they are still in the process of learning English," Draculaura remarked before muttering under her breath, "and, from the looks of it, nail and hair care as well."

Trolls, especially older ones such as these, were exceptionally good at maintaining order *except* where their physical appearance was concerned. They wholeheartedly refused to cut both their hair (and, sadly, that included nose hair) and their claws. But perhaps most egregious, they refused to bathe more than once every fortnight—hence the thick layer of brown grime atop their skin.

The new teacher stepped up to the microphone as Frankie and Draculaura moved aside. "Hello, lovely ghouls," Miss Flapper uttered in a soft yet raspy voice, which enraptured all within earshot. "I am so honored to be here with you, though I do, of course, miss my colleagues and students in Bitealy. However, they were kind enough to send this amazing cavalry of trolls with me. They are not only expert hall monitors but also wild-dragon wranglers. I certainly hope you find them as delightful and charming as I do."

Miss Flapper's silky tone was exquisitely matched by her captivating physical beauty. With iridescent skin, a heart-shaped mouth, blazing green eyes, and long bloodred hair, the woman was absolutely breathtaking. And like all European dragons, she had not a scale or tail in sight. She was dressed head to toe in couture, skillfully tailored to fit around her delicate off-white wings.

"Talk about the bee's knees! That woman is gorgeous," Robecca murmured quietly.

"I wonder what she uses to exfoliate," Rochelle pondered while self-consciously rubbing her hard granite legs. "Her skin looks so soft."

"I can't believe she's a wild-dragon whisperer. They're usually all burned and crispy after years of accidents and whatnot," Venus muttered as Frankie Stein once again took to the podium.

"As many of you know, we are fast approaching the Dance of the Delightfully Dead. And here to tell you more about this year's plans are reigning Scream Queen and King, Cleo de Nile and Deuce Gorgon."

The crowd cheered loudly as a mummirific Egyptian princess with coffee-colored skin and black-and-gold tresses took to the stage. Walking immediately behind her was a handsome boy sporting sunglasses and a snake-hawk—a Mohawk of snakes.

"Hey, kids. Cleo here, with my boyfriend, Deuce. As usual, the Dance of the Delightfully Dead will be held the day after quarterly exams, at Salem's oldest cemetery, the Skelemoanian. It's the most important event of the year, so please dress accordingly. In other words, no matted fur, no yellow fangs, and definitely no dried scales."

"Party starts promptly at eleven PM and ends at sunrise," Deuce said before being rammed to the side by Miss Sue Nami, who knocked his glasses askew in the process.

And before Deuce was able to slip them back over his eyes, a troll wandered directly into his line of vision. The oily little creature instantly turned to stone, prompting Deuce to grunt in frustration. "Not again!"

"Per the schedule, the assembly is now over. All nonadult entities are to exit in a single-file line," Miss Sue Nami instructed before shaking herself like a wet dog. "Class schedules are being e-mailed to you at this very moment. If you do not have an iCoffin phone, make friends with someone who does and then use that person's device to check your e-mail."

A crush of monsters filled the halls, all excitedly checking their iCoffins.

"Dear me!" Robecca babbled as she bumped into her new dorm neighbor, Cy Clops, causing her knee gear to squeak loudly. "Oops, sorry about that! Clearly it's time for an oil change!"

"Crowds can be very dangerous," Rochelle explained seriously. "Monsters often wind up with broken claws, bruised paws, or pulled fur."

"Um, it's a bunch of teenagers, not Transylvania during a full moon. I think we can handle it," Venus replied.

"While you may choose to ignore a gargoyle's warning, a gargoyle must never choose to ignore an opportunity to warn," Rochelle said primly.

"Is that from a fortune cookie?" Venus scoffed, pulling her iCoffin from her recycled book bag.

"Absolutely not. Gargoyles do not believe in either fortune-tellers or fortune cookies," Rochelle replied seriously. "We do, however, really like Chinese food."

"Isn't this swell? We're in all the same classes!" Robecca said excitedly while comparing iCoffins.

"Yeah, but we didn't get Dragon Whispering 101," Venus grumbled. "I'm really disappointed. Reptiles love me."

"Not me. I've never been too fond of whispering. It seems to me people only whisper when they're saying things they shouldn't be saying," Robecca explained.

"Hey, are you guys new?" Frankie Stein approached the trio, with a zombie walking slowly behind her.

"Is it that obvious?" Venus replied.

"Well, you're the only ones left in the hall except the trolls. I'm Frankie Stein, by the way, and this is Ghoulia Yelps."

"Grrrrnnn," Ghoulia mumbled, much to the confusion of Venus.

"I'm guessing that you don't speak zombie," Frankie said.

Venus shrugged.

"*Bonjour*," Rochelle jumped in. "I am Rochelle Goyle, and this is Robecca Steam and Venus McFlytrap. We're roommates in the new dorm."

"That's so voltage! You'll love it here! Let me know if you guys need anything."

"By any chance do you know how to get to Ghoulish Literature with Dr. Clamdestine?"

Rochelle inquired, reading the details off her iCoffin.

"That's in the Libury—straight ahead, turn right at the tombstone and left at the mounted horn. Good luck!" Frankie called out before making her way down the hall with Ghoulia following in her wake.

CHAPTER

five

the Libury was a cold and drafty place filled with dust bunnies, creaky furniture, and the greatest monster stories ever told. Organized by species, the tales featured or were written by every type of creature imaginable, from the popular to the obscure. These volumes were more than just Ghoulish Literature; they were Monstory—the history of monsters as told by the creatures themselves.

Dr. Clamdestine entered the Libury just as the bell clanged, signifying the start of class. Dressed in a tweed suit with dark brown patches at the elbows and carrying a large leather satchel, the middle-aged sea monster definitely looked the part of literature professor, albeit one with a faint whiff of salt water.

"Students," Dr. Clamdestine greeted the class before dramatically lowering his head for a thirty-second period of silence. After which he pulled a pipe from his jacket pocket and continued. "I find cleansing my mental palate very helpful before diving into Ghoulish Literature."

"*Pardonnez-moi*, Dr. Clamdestine, but smoking is definitely not allowed at Monster High. Plus, it is very, very bad for you," Rochelle stated firmly.

"And *us*. It totally makes me wilt," Venus whispered to Rochelle.

"This isn't a pipe, young gargoyle. It may look like a pipe, but it is definitely not a pipe. In actuality, it is a well-carved hunk of cheese, one that I will likely eat for lunch later. You see, teaching is very similar to acting; both professions use props to aid in the accessing of different characters. And this cheese pipe is currently helping me access my intellectual persona, the great Dr. Clamdestine."

"Dear me, I think that sounds a lot more like a circus performer than a teacher," Robecca muttered to Venus and Rochelle.

"Now then, for my monologue, also known as roll call," Dr. Clamdestine said while putting away his cheese pipe and pulling out a clipboard. "Lagoona Blue? Draculaura? Jackson Jekyll or Holt Hyde? Deuce Gorgon?"

As the names of her classmates echoed throughout the room, Rochelle eyed the eternally sunglasses-clad Deuce Gorgon. She found him both handsome and intriguing. Perhaps it was because he wasn't crafted out of granite or because she was one of the few people at school who might one day look into his eyes. Since she was already made of stone, Deuce's Gorgon snake stare posed no threat to her.

69

"Cleo de Nile?" Dr. Clamdestine continued.

Upon hearing the name of Deuce's girlfriend, Rochelle quickly snapped out of her haze, remembering that she too was taken! Why, only a few days earlier in Scaris, she had said good-bye to her lovable gargoyle boyfriend, Garrott. Just thinking about Garrott filled her with overwhelming guilt.

While Rochelle pondered the moral implications of her burgeoning crush, Venus sat next to her, seething with rage over Cleo de Nile's large collection of shopping bags.

"Look at all those paper bags! It's down-right irresponsible. She's basically a tree killer," Venus spouted angrily to Robecca and Rochelle.

"Jeez Louise, Venus, don't you think 'tree

killer' is a bit harsh? Maybe she just forgot her reusable shopping bag at home. I forget things all the time," Robecca squeaked, hoping to appease Venus's growing environmental rage.

But Venus was not the type of monster who was easily placated. And before Robecca knew it, Venus was waving her light green arms in the air, desperate to garner Cleo's attention.

"Hey, Cleo, over here. The name's Venus. I'm new to Monster High."

"Welcome," Cleo responded frostily.

"It looks like you did some serious back-to-school shopping this morning. That must have been a lot of fun. But do you know what would have been even more fun? Bringing your own reusable bag to the Maul and saving a tree's life!"

"Why are you talking to me about my bags and trees and stuff? Do I look like a forest ranger or garbage collector to you?"

"I'll have you know that those are two of the noblest professions in the world. They are on the front lines every day fighting antienvironmentalists like you! Do you even realize that we need trees to produce oxygen?" Venus declared as her vines curled tightly around her fists.

"*Fight like you're right! Fight with all your might!*" a lone pumpkin head sang from his perch in the corner of the room.

"Way to spaz out, *weed*," Cleo replied before turning to Clawdeen Wolf. "She is definitely not Fearleading or Frightingale material."

The Frightingale Society was the school's all-girls social club—a literal who's who of teenage monsters and, as such, very hard to get into.

"Ah, mate," Lagoona Blue exclaimed in her bubbly Australian accent, "she's just trying to keep the world healthy for all of us."

"Whatever," Cleo replied as Venus's face

continued to grow redder with rage.

"Venus, I'm concerned about your blood pressure; you look like you're about to explode. I would advise you to continue this conversation later," Rochelle interjected.

"The *planet* cannot wait for *later*!" Venus professed while dramatically flinging her hands in the air, green vines flailing about wildly.

"How about I see you *later*? Or better yet, *never*?" Cleo answered cuttingly.

Venus's nose twitched and her cheeks bulged before she expelled a most thunderous sneeze. The bright orange cloud of pollen descended upon Cleo de Nile, miraculously missing any of the surrounding students.

"Babe, are you okay? Are your clothes okay?" Deuce asked sweetly, worried that Cleo might be more distressed about the state of her clothing than anything else.

73

"Of course I am," Cleo said with uncharacteristic warmth and kindness before turning to Venus. "Thank you for showing me the error of my ways. You're absolutely right; it is irresponsible to shop without a reusable bag. As a matter of fact, I am going to commission a solid gold bag that will last forever! Thank you, Venus, thank you!"

"A solid gold bag would be very heavy, nearly impossible to carry," Rochelle mumbled to herself.

Deuce then sweetly put his hand on Cleo's forehead. "Babe, you're really freaking me out right now. Are you sure you're not upset about being sneezed on?"

Having watched the drama unfold as if it were a theatrical production staged for his enjoyment, Dr. Clamdestine finally decided it was time to step in.

"Let me guess. Venus McFlytrap?"

"Yes, that's me, Dr. Clamdestine."

"Pollens of persuasion are strictly prohibited at school."

"I know. I'm really sorry," Venus said with discernible regret. She couldn't believe she had lost control of her pollens so soon after arriving at Monster High.

"As a connoisseur of drama, I appreciate your passion. However, as a teacher, I cannot allow you to use your pollens of persuasion without repercussions," Dr. Clamdestine explained. He then called into the hall, "Troll? Troll? Would the closest troll please come to the Libury?"

Within seconds, an extraordinarily chubby gray-haired troll with a pulsating red nose waddled into the room. After looking around for a few seconds, the troll followed Dr. Clamdestine's gaze directly to Venus McFlytrap. The troll then toddled over to Venus, promptly wiped his nose on his hand, and motioned for her to follow him into the hall.

75

"*Bon chance*," Rochelle whispered while waving her pink-monogrammed handkerchief in the air.

"Don't let him eat you," Robecca added.

"I wouldn't worry about that," a quiet voice came from behind Robecca. "Trolls are vegetarians."

It was Cy Clops, and as usual the shy boy was staring at the ground with his arms awkwardly crossed.

"Good golly, that is good to know, thank you," Robecca replied, to which the boy merely nodded his head.

Once in the main corridor, the troll again used his grimy hand as a tissue. It was a visually arresting sight, one that prompted Venus to look down at the purple-checkered floor in disgust.

"Do you know what I do whenever I have a cold? Swallow loads of vitamin C, drink plenty of fluids, and—here is the most important part—only blow my nose with handkerchiefs. This will not only help you get better but also help you socially. Because if there is one thing that turns off potential friends, it's booger-encrusted hands."

"No time. You must listen. Bad thing here," the troll grunted quietly.

"Is that your way of saying I have detention?"

"Bad thing here, ruin school," the troll yammered on before looking around suspiciously.

"I don't understand."

"Happen before. Now bad thing here. You must listen. Stop bad thing."

"I'm sorry, I don't understand Trollish. I have no idea what you are trying to tell me."

"Too late," the elderly red-nosed creature whispered before ducking into a passing pack of trolls.

CHAPTER Six

mr. Hackington, aka Mr. Hack, was perhaps the school's most unpleasant-looking teacher, with his metal mask, oversized chin, and pointy, elf-like ears. He was a mad scientist who rather appropriately taught Mad Science in the Absolutely Deranged Scientist Laboratory, a room brimming with Bunsen burners, microscopes, and vials of potent potions. With a keen understanding of the recklessness that comes with being a teenager, Mr. Hack kept all treacherous liquids under lock and key.

"Botany—the study of plants—is one of my favorite sections, for it allows me to teach homeopathic zombification," Mr. Hack  explained before breaking into hysterical laughter. "Now then, does anyone know what Burnwidth Serum turns into when heated to one hundred degrees Fahrenheit?"

"Really hot Burnwidth Serum?" Henry Hunchback joked.

"Mr. Hack doesn't like jokes," Hoodude whispered while scribbling Frankie Stein's name on the front of his notebook.

"That's pathetic, Hunchback," Mr. Hack replied harshly.

A trio of pumpkin heads at the back of the class sang quietly, *"What serum? What serum? I wish I could hear him!"*

"What about you, McFlytrap? You're a plant. Surely you must know all about the derivatives of the Burnwidth Bush?"

"Um, um, um . . ." Venus mumbled, literally wilting under her teacher's intent gaze.

"It turns into a zombification serum for cold-blooded creatures," said a quiet voice.

"You are correct, Clops," Mr. Hack said excitedly before smashing a metal tray against the counter and laughing intensely. "I love hearing the right answer!"

"What a well-oiled mind that Cyclops must have! How else could he know such a thing?" Robecca wondered while looking over at the painfully shy boy.

"Maybe he was raised by botanists. Or perhaps he spends his free time reading Monsterpedia," Rochelle hypothesized. "It's impossible to say for sure."

As Robecca continued to stare at Cy, Henry leaned over and patted the one-eyed boy on the back.

"Nice. It's always good to have a roommate to cheat off! Hey, I've been meaning to ask you—are you trying out for the Skulltimate Roller Maze team?"

"No, I don't think so," Cy said, squirming under Robecca's gaze.

"But it's the most fun you'll ever have!"

At that exact moment, Robecca caught Cy's one eye and smiled in a friendly manner, igniting a rush of adrenaline in the boy.

"Come on, what do you say?" Henry pressed.

"What? Okay, sure, whatever," Cy babbled, unaware of what he was even agreeing to.

"Excellent! I think you'll really like the team captain, Clawd Wolf. He's a real howl."

After Mad Science came Home Ick and finally Physical Deaducation. Much to Cy's delight, Robecca too had decided to join the Skulltimate Roller Maze team. But then she was, after all, one of the founders of the game, back in the eighteenth century, before she was dismantled. Rochelle, while a very good Roller Maze player, decided to stay put with Venus in Graveyard Dancing. Both girls were quite keen to learn the mumba (the mummies' take on the rumba).

Dimly lit, with countless pathways crafted of thick and prickly hedges, the maze was a vast space that seemed to trick the mind at every turn. The tall and neatly manicured bushes lulled newcomers into a false sense of safety, masking the enormity of the arena. Bats perched atop bars just below the ceiling acted as camera crew, documenting the players' every move. And while most of the labyrinth was neatly maintained, Headmistress Bloodgood treated more than a few pockets like de facto storage units, filled with old desks and rusted contraptions. But then again, the maze was only used for practice; official games were played elsewhere.

Ever the daredevil, Robecca threw herself into Skulltimate Roller Maze training without so much as a second thought. Within minutes, she was buzzing through the dark green hedges, courtesy of her special rocket boots, occasionally even stopping to perform aerial stunts. Robecca's ability to fly over the maze and rescue bewildered teammates made her an instant favorite.

Hours later, long after the bell had clanged to signal the end of Physical Deaducation, Robecca abruptly dashed out of the maze. With her rocket boots still smoking, she stormed into the main corridor, desperate to find someone with a watch or an iCoffin. Robecca had rather unfortunately left her iCoffin in one of her previous classes, but she hadn't a clue which one.

"Oh, please! Tell me, what time is it? I'm late!" Robecca exclaimed as she saw Frankie Stein and her werewolf friend Clawdeen Wolf making their way down the main hall.

"Hey, what's the hurry?" Frankie asked sweetly as Clawdeen stepped back, away from Robecca.

"Sorry! You're steaming, and I don't want to get fur frizz. You understand, right?"

"Oh, of course! Fur frizz is the absolute flea's

sneeze! But tell me, do you know what time it is? I'm sure I'm late for something. I just can't remember what!"

As Frankie looked at her watch, a small and quiet voice came as if out of nowhere. "Five PM."

It was Cy Clops, and he was holding a terribly sour-faced Penny the penguin.

"I think you forgot someone in the maze," he said shyly as he lowered Penny to the ground before quickly scurrying off.

"Dear me! Penny, I am so sorry!" Robecca babbled at her mechanical pet.

"Hey, the Frightingale Society is about to have its first meeting of the year, if you and your roomies are interested. It's sort of like a sorority. We do all kinds of stuff together, everything from learning monster etiquette to getting manicures—or, in some cases, clawdicures," Frankie said.

"Thank you, Frankie. That really does sound

swell, but Rochelle and I wouldn't want to join without Venus. And, well, let's just say Venus and Cleo's relationship could use a steam cleaning."

"Oh, of course, the infamous sneeze," Clawdeen said while nodding her head in recognition. "You know mummies—they can really hold a grudge."

Rochelle sighed as she watched the two girls walk away. She couldn't wait to start joining clubs at Monster High!

CHAPTER
seven

at lunch the following day, Monster High's Creepateria was absolutely abuzz with stories of the amazing, stylish, supernaturally interesting Miss Flapper. Why, even Spectra Vondergeist, everyone's favorite purple-haired ghost, was posting about the new teacher on her blog, *Ghostly Gossip*! It was as if the entire student body, both boys and girls, had developed an all-consuming crush on the newest member of the staff. Well, maybe not the entire school. Venus, Robecca, and Rochelle were far too focused on another member of the faculty to mind Miss Flapper.

"There is no point mincing words: Clearly an intervention is needed!" Rochelle exclaimed while tapping her fingers repeatedly on the wooden tabletop, dimpling the surface.

"An intervention for what?" Venus asked reasonably.

"For depression, of course! *Regardez!* He's trying to drown himself in his soup!"

Venus rolled her eyes at Rochelle before realizing that Mr. D'eath was, in fact, trying to submerge his bony face in two inches of split pea soup.

"Okay, let's not overreact. He's eating lunch with Miss Sue Nami. I think we can all agree that spending time with that woman would make anyone a little crazy," Venus assessed.

"Just look at his clothes! Only a man with nothing to live for would go out in such an outfit. Plus, when he yawned earlier, I noticed his teeth were looking a bit gray. And everyone knows that once skeletons stop whitening their teeth, they've hit rock bottom."

"Who told you that? Your dentist?" Venus asked incredulously.

"I bet gargoyles make wonderful dentists," Robecca asserted earnestly.

"It's true, we do. We don't even have to use instruments; we can do it all with our pinkie fingers," Rochelle said proudly before pausing to watch Miss Sue Nami.

The soggy woman, whose profile closely

91

resembled an overstuffed trash can, awkwardly leaped out of her chair, arms flailing. Sitting for extended periods of time led to waterlogging and, on rare occasions, flooding. And so as a flabby-faced troll removed her tray from the table, Miss Sue Nami began aggressively shaking, moving every body part from her toes to her scalp. Unfortunately for Mr. D'eath, his lunch, and the troll, these motions created a heavy shower—not that Miss Sue Nami acknowledged it, let alone apologized for her behavior.

"Per paragraph 7.9 of the Gargoyle Code of Ethics: Once a gargoyle has decided to help, actions should be both focused and speedy," Rochelle announced before throwing down her napkin and walking over to Mr. D'eath.

And while it was not the most graceful of walks, since Rochelle was rather heavy-footed when excited, it clearly conveyed the intensity she felt regarding the gloom-stricken man.

"*Bonjour*, Monsieur D'eath. My name is Rochelle Goyle, and I am a new student from Scaris."

"Scaris? I've always wanted to go there—walk along the river, eat smelly cheese, maybe even wear a beret."

"I'm not sure a beret would suit you, but I think you'd definitely enjoy our smelly cheese," Rochelle said in her usual matter-of-fact manner.

"It doesn't really matter. I'll never make it to Scaris. I might as well add it to the list now," Mr. D'eath said with a sigh.

"*Pardonnez-moi?* What list are you talking about?" Rochelle inquired.

"The regret list. It's a comprehensive record of all the things I plan on regretting right before I die. I only hope my death isn't too sudden—I've got a lot to go over."

"I'm sorry if I am being impolite, but aren't you already dead?"

"That is technically correct. But I'm talking about the death of my soul."

"That is heavy, Monsieur D'eath."

"I get that a lot," he grumbled.

"Actually, so do I, but for different reasons," Rochelle said, looking down at her slender yet weighty frame. "Monsieur D'eath, I was wondering if I might revamp your wardrobe, help you liven things up a bit. Not that there is anything wrong with your stained brown trousers and pilled brown sweater."

"Students aren't allowed to get involved in teachers' personal lives."

"And is that an actual rule or more of a suggestion?" Rochelle asked.

"It's not technically a rule, just sort of an accepted thing. Now, if you'll excuse me, I really

94

should get back to wallowing in self-pity; I haven't done nearly enough of it today."

"I hold rules in very high regard and thus clearly delineate between actual rules and suggestions. And as this is not a real rule, we would not be doing anything wrong. Therefore, I insist we move forward."

"Okay," Mr. D'eath mumbled, "but we'll have to stop if my pessimism starts rubbing off on you. After all, misery and youth do not belong together."

"Clearly, there is much you do not understand about youth," Rochelle mumbled to herself before holding out her small gray hand for Mr. D'eath to shake. "And please excuse the coldness of my skin. It comes with being carved from granite."

"Please excuse my personality. It comes with being me."

CHAPTER eight

s night fell over Monster High, the bats awoke eager to hunt. After a full day's rest, they wanted nothing more than to gorge themselves on insects and spiders. With perked ears and open mouths, they swooped through the halls, flapping ferociously.

On the second floor of the east wing, Monster High's boarders prepared for bed. Blanche and Rose Van Sangre, true to their gypsy roots, pulled the sheets off their beds and set up camp under a pine tree on the back lawn. The pumpkin heads, exhausted from an active day of singing and gossiping, were already fast asleep, with their bullfrogs snoring beside them. Three-Headed Freddie was nodding off while reading three different editions of the *New Yuck Times* bestselling book *Crisis in the Middle Beast*. Hoodude was, as usual, looking at pictures of Frankie Stein and fiddling with his pins. Henry Hunchback lay in bed dissecting Miss Sylphia Flapper's exquisite beauty while Cy reminisced about a certain steam-inclined young girl.

"Today really was the absolute bee's knees! I honestly can't remember a better day. Well, except for the part where I forgot Penny," Robecca said as she looked at the pajama-clad penguin sleeping next to her. "Thank heavens she doesn't hold a grudge!"

"Actually, I'm quite sure she does. I think that's why she always looks so grumpy," Rochelle interrupted. "Or maybe I just think she's grumpy because compared to Roux, everyone's grumpy!"

"Ouch, Chewy! Watch the fingers," Venus squealed. "By the way, I don't know if I mentioned this already, but I wouldn't leave any jewelry lying out. Chewy has been known to swallow an earring or two. But don't worry—all very inexpensive stuff. He seems to prefer gold-plated. I guess it's easier to digest."

"Speaking of eating, I heard the trolls are vegetarians! So no need to worry about them devouring us for tardiness," Robecca said, stifling a yawn.

"I had a seriously weird encounter with that troll yesterday in Dr. Clamdestine's class."

"I still can't believe he didn't give you detention," Robecca added.

"He was freaking out about something, but I couldn't understand a single word he said," Venus remarked as she replayed the meeting in her mind.

"Well, they are quite elderly trolls. Or perhaps they're not up to date on their rabies vaccinations; incoherent babbling is a very common sign of infection. I will definitely have to look into this," Rochelle said firmly before turning over to sleep.

The sun had barely risen, when Robecca bolted straight out of bed like a madwoman. Steam puffed from both her ears and her nose, instantly frizzing her hair, as she darted back and forth across the room. Tucked tightly under her left arm was a still-slumbering, pajama-clad Penny.

"Good golly, Miss Molly! What time is it?

What have I missed? Where's Penny?" Robecca babbled, her brain clearly still half asleep.

"Robecca! *Qu'est-ce que tu fais?* It's six thirty in the morning!"

"Deary me! I woke up absolutely sure I had slept through half the day."

"You haven't even slept through half the morning, so why don't you go back to bed?" Venus said groggily from beneath the shreds of her organic-cotton mummy gauze sleep mask.

"Now, why in the name of the mouse's house would I do that? Then I'd definitely be late. This way I might actually be on time for a change. I think I'll take Penny out for an early-morning gear grease and then meet you guys at the Creepateria in an hour."

The second the door slammed shut, Rochelle's intuition told her she wouldn't see Robecca again for ages. For no matter how much time Robecca had, it would never be enough. She simply wasn't wired for punctuality. Why, if Rochelle weren't a levelheaded gargoyle, she might have wondered if being late was Robecca's destiny. Was it possible that Robecca's life was supposed to unfold an hour or two later than scheduled?

True to form, two hours later Robecca had missed both breakfast and the morning assembly. Standing at the front of the Vampitheater and scanning the crowd for her missing roommate, Rochelle spotted a familiar miserable face.

"*Bonjour*, Monsieur D'eath."

"Rochelle," he mumbled while keeping his eyes glued to the floor.

"Did you get the Abnerzombie and Witch catalog I left on your desk? I thought you might enjoy seeing some of the latest fashions."

"I enjoyed getting a gift," Mr. D'eath said with a sigh. "I've never gotten one before."

Rochelle was shaking her head sadly when a nearby kerfuffle grabbed her attention. While exiting the Creepateria, Deuce Gorgon had tumbled atop a pimpled troll, sending both of them straight to the ground. Without thinking or even knowing what she was doing, Rochelle dropped her bag and dashed frantically to Deuce.

"Deuce! Boo la la! Are you okay?" Rochelle inquired with genuine affection.

"Yeah, I think I'm fine," Deuce said with a smile before lifting his head and looking straight into Rochelle's eyes.

"You have such beautiful green eyes. They are absolutely *fangtastique*," Rochelle babbled from her fog of infatuation. "They even match the snakes on your head."

"My glasses!" Deuce screeched. He covered his eyes and began feeling around the floor.

"They're right here," Rochelle said as she placed them in Deuce's hand.

"I'm pretty lucky you were the first person I saw. Turning people into stone is not very popular around here."

"I think I'm the lucky one—to have seen your eyes, that is," Rochelle prattled. "I'm quite sure you're the most handsome man I've ever seen. If I were you, I would just stare in the mirror all day."

Venus suddenly threw her arm around Rochelle and inserted herself into the fast-declining conversation about Deuce's beauty.

"Hey, Deuce, Rochelle just had a root canal, so she has no idea what she's saying. Earlier today she asked my pet plant to marry her."

"I most definitely did not, but I am rather certain that Chewy ate my antique watch this

104

morning. There was a notable ticking sound coming from his pot," Rochelle stated as Venus attempted to cover her friend's mouth with vines.

"Well, we'd better get go—" Venus began to mumble.

"I didn't think gargoyles could get cavities," Deuce interjected.

"Only Scarisian gargoyles can," Venus fibbed poorly. "It's from . . . eating all that smelly cheese. A lot of people don't realize it, but smelly cheese is really bad for your teeth."

"That is empirically false," Rochelle asserted after freeing her mouth of vines. "Smelly cheese has absolutely no effect on your teeth. And Deuce, you are correct; gargoyles cannot get cavities. We are, however, highly susceptible to grinding our teeth, which is why most gargoyles—my pet, Roux, included—wear night guards."

Deuce immediately erupted in a fit of laughter.

"You guys are a riot," he declared before wandering off.

"Thanks. Yeah, this whole thing is just material from our comedy routine," Venus called after him.

"We do not have a comedy routine. And I should mention that gargoyles are not well known for their sense of humor," Rochelle corrected Venus.

"What is wrong with you? I was trying to help! Do you even realize that you told Deuce you were lucky to look into his eyes? That if you were him, you would stay home all day looking at yourself in the mirror? It was as if a soap-opera character hijacked your brain! And not a good one. A really embarrassing one who says things like 'I love you, Victor Marcoplis, and I'll make you mine if it kills me' while looking directly into the camera."

"Your parents let you watch too much television as a child."

"Or maybe yours didn't let you watch enough," Venus shot back while fixing her tangled vines.

"Let's debate this another time. We're going to be late for Home Ick if we wait any longer for Robecca."

"I think we should reconsider my idea of putting Robecca on a leash. It really is for her own good."

"She's not a bullfrog," Rochelle responded, immediately thinking of the pumpkin heads' pets.

"You do realize that bullfrogs don't normally walk on leashes? That trio of pumpkin heads is just really weird," Venus explained as they started down the crowded hall, heading directly into a flurry of excitement.

107

miss Flapper frolicked effortlessly down the purple-and-green corridor. The nimble-footed European was leading a bevy of trolls who themselves were walking small green dragons, each no larger than an average house cat. The unusually delicate Miss Flapper appeared almost to be walking on air, so light and feminine was her step. Dressed head to toe in white Scaremès couture, the woman floated from student to student, whispering in their ears. And while no one could hear what she was saying, it must have been terribly intense. The students'

faces momentarily flashed blank before morphing back to normal.

"What do you suppose Miss Flapper is whispering to them?" Venus asked Rochelle as a pod of pumpkin heads knocked against her in their pursuit of the popular teacher.

"Although this is purely conjecture, it's possible she is informing them of the trolls' dubious Bitealian vaccination records."

"*Miss Flapper is so pretty, like a perfect Persian kitty*," Sam, James, and Marvin the pumpkin heads sang loudly upon presenting themselves to their teacher.

"Oh, pumpkin heads," Miss Flapper purred in her soft yet raspy voice, "it's such a shame you're not in my class. You really must join my after-school club, the Monster Advancement League League. We added the extra *league* so that we might call ourselves MALL," Miss Flapper said before leaning in to whisper in their ears.

With a self-satisfied smile, the beguiling woman continued down the corridor, whispering to everyone from Draculaura to Cleo de Nile, until she found herself face-to-face with Rochelle. Miss Flapper leaned in slowly, her rose perfume instantly reminding the petite gargoyle of Garrott and the amazing rosebush he had created in her honor. However, just as the woman parted her perfect pink lips to whisper in Rochelle's ear, a voice cut through the hall, causing the young gargoyle to turn her head abruptly.

"Deary me! I'm late again!" Robecca's voice echoed through the corridor.

"She's baaack," Venus drawled, and Miss Flapper moved on, making her way toward Ghoulia Yelps.

"In the name of the mouse's house, I haven't a clue what happened to me!" Robecca called out loudly while crossing the busy corridor to Venus and Rochelle.

As always seemed to happen, the steam-ridden Robecca bumped into Cy Clops amid the throng of students. Unfortunately, her metal plates were still sweltering, making the collision more than a little painful for the one-eyed boy.

"*Ouch!*"

"Sorry!" she cried.

"Quiet in hall! *Quiet!*" a troll yelled.

"But I'm late! Surely that is a worse offense than talking loudly!" Robecca protested.

"Go class or I eat you!" the troll countered angrily.

"Oh, stop bluffing. I know you're a vegetarian," Robecca retorted.

"Hello? I'm a plant," Venus replied while pulling Robecca away. "Hurry up or we're going to miss Home Ick."

"*Je ne comprends pas!* Why are you always late?" a confused Rochelle asked Robecca.

"Deary me, I've thought about it so many times, though I'm still not sure I know the answer. My best guess is that I get so caught up in things that I forget everything else, and then, like a lightning bolt, this feeling hits. And I know I'm late, but I don't know for what because I haven't a clue what time it is."

"But you're wearing a watch. Several, in fact," Rochelle countered.

"Yes, but they don't work. Steam kills watches. I only wear them because I think they're awfully stylish."

"Well, at least you *have* a watch," Rochelle said, shooting Venus a knowing look.

113

"Welcome to Home Ick," Miss Kindergrubber announced impatiently as she looked around the class. "What a sad sight! The lot of you is nothing but skin and bones," the haggard old witch, garbed in a patchwork dress and worn head scarf, declared. "Well, lucky for you we are making a delicious stew today—one of the world's most famous Dragonian recipes, Crispy Tongue Soup. And before you ask, no, it does not actually contain a tongue! Oh, hello, Robecca dear."

"Excuse me, Miss Kindergrubber, but since none of us are dragons, wouldn't it make more sense to cook something else?" Venus asked with some distaste.

"Excuse me, child, but I never said you had to be a fire-breather to enjoy it! But, of course, this soup is rather irresistible to dragons," the woman replied curtly while pulling a large pot out from under the counter and opening her enormous leather-bound cookbook.

The process of making Crispy Tongue Soup was actually rather difficult—or at least Miss Kindergrubber made it seem that way, groaning anytime anyone asked a question or mismeasured an ingredient. As Robecca dropped witch hazel into her pot, Cy watched her every move. He was seated directly behind her so that he could see her as clearly as possible; like all Cyclopes, he had trouble with peripheral vision and depth perception.

"You know, my head may be in front of my belly button, but even I can see that you've got something for that steamer," Henry Hunchback teased Cy.

"I don't know what you're talking about," Cy said dismissively before returning his eye to his bubbling pot. "And don't call her a steamer; her name is Robecca."

"I rest my case," Henry offered with an innocent laugh.

As the end of class neared, Miss Kindergrubber tasted all the students' work before revealing that Three-Headed Freddie had most success-fully executed the recipe. And while no one said it aloud, more than one student thought the boy had an unfair advantage, considering he had two more brains than the average monster.

"I am very impressed, Three-Headed Freddie,"

Miss Kindergrubber said honestly. "I would serve this to the finest dragons I know."

"*Merci boo-coup*, thank you, *grazie*," Three-Headed Freddie replied with evident pride.

Upon laying down their ladles, the trio of pumpkin heads promptly began passing out flyers for the Monster Advancement League League while singing indiscreetly and off-key about gossip they heard in the hall. *"Frankie Stein thinks MALL is divine. Says Cleo de Nile, the club will make you smile."*

"James?" Rochelle called to the pumpkin head. "What exactly do you do at this club?"

"*We prance, we dance, we help monsters advance*," the pumpkin head sang flatly in response.

"Not to be rude, but that is awfully vague. Might you give me a few specifics?"

"*If we put monsters first, the world will no*

longer be cursed. Now, if you'll excuse me, I'm absolutely dying of thirst."

"That made no sense," Venus mumbled to Rochelle. "Well, except the part about being thirsty. I sure could use a good watering about now."

Later that afternoon, long after school had finished, Rochelle called a most important meeting in their dorm room.

"*Je suis tellement excitée,*" Rochelle said as Roux played by her feet. "Are you ready?"

"Oh yes! I'm positively pleased as punch not to be missing this unveiling!" Robecca said while holding up a silk scarf linking her right arm to Venus's left.

"I had a feeling you'd like the leash once you got used to it," Venus said proudly.

118

"Absolutely, and so does Penny," Robecca said, looking down at her cantankerous pet penguin, currently tied to her left boot.

"I really hope you guys like it and, of course, that Monsieur D'eath likes it," Rochelle said with an excited smile. The young gargoyle then pulled a stringy yellow mess out from behind her back. "*Et voilà!*"

"Is that a hat?" Venus asked in all seriousness.

"What? No, it's a suit. Can't you tell?"

"Well, I can definitely tell that you sewed it yourself," Venus replied.

"I wanted it to be *très monsterfique*, something truly special," Rochelle explained.

"Well, I suppose it depends on your definition of special," Robecca replied diplomatically.

"*Zut!* It's that bad?" Rochelle asked with palpable disappointment.

"It looks like it was shredded by a pack of feral

119

cats," Venus proclaimed bluntly.

"Venus," Robecca snapped, "isn't that a bit harsh?"

"No, she's right. Every time I touched it, my claws snagged a string, then another and another, and before I knew it, I had wasted twelve yards of fabric creating this!"

"Dear Rochelle, why didn't you ask us for help?" Robecca asked sweetly.

"Paragraph 3.5 of the Gargoyle Code of Ethics states, 'Do not ask others to do for you what you can do for yourself.'"

"But you *can't* do it for yourself. Surely that much is clear," Venus pointed out. "Seriously, it's almost tragic what you did to that poor, defenseless piece of cloth!"

Rochelle lowered her head in shame; she couldn't believe she had actually thought she could pull this off.

"Don't look so sad. In case you forgot, we go to school with one of the finest seamstresses in Oregon."

"Venus, I can sew a button or two, but I'm better with rivets," Robecca replied.

"Not you, Robecca! I'm talking about Frankie Stein. She sews her own body parts together. I'm sure she can handle a suit."

"Do you think she'd do it?" Rochelle wondered aloud.

"It doesn't hurt to ask," Robecca responded with a smile.

"That isn't technically true. It can, in fact, hurt to ask. I can give you multiple examples if you'd like," Rochelle clarified.

"I don't think that's going to be necessary. Come on, ghouls, grab your stuff. We have a green monster to find," Venus announced as she opened the door.

121

"But school's already over for the day," Robecca said.

Venus smiled. "Yes, which is exactly why we're heading into town."

As the trio made their way down the dormitory corridor, Rochelle noticed a decline in the quality of the delicate webbed curtain. When she paused to check on the spiders, she noted that at least half of the quarter-sized black creatures had vanished.

"What are you looking at?" Robecca asked Rochelle.

"The spiders. Many of them seem to have disappeared."

"Maybe they're on vacation," Venus interjected quickly—a little too quickly for Rochelle's liking.

"Have you been letting Chewlian into the hall?" Rochelle inquired accusingly.

"I have no idea what you're talking about,"

Venus poorly covered before bolting down the pink staircase.

Upon stepping into the main corridor, Robecca was met by a familiar sight: Cy Clops. She couldn't help noticing that the boy was absolutely everywhere. Why, she nearly saw him more than Venus and Rochelle, and she lived with them!

As the threesome made their way toward the front entrance, Robecca asked casually, "Have you noticed that boy Cy Clops hanging around a lot?"

"Well, he does live in the dormitory with us," Venus said with a hint of sarcasm as she pulled open the gargantuan door.

The center of town was a ten-minute walk from Monster High's campus. The quaint and charming village of Salem had the two things teenagers

123

needed and loved most: a Maul and a Coffin Bean coffee shop that served the yummiest milk shakes!

Rochelle, Venus, and Robecca began their search for Frankie at the Maul, scanning every store they passed for even the faintest hint of green. And although the three friends were highly focused on finding Frankie, they gave themselves a short break to check out the latest fashions in Transylvania's Secret. Rochelle, who had never been in a Transylvania's Secret before, was impressed with the cutting-edge fashion and made a mental note to return once the Mr. D'eath mission was complete.

After searching every inch of the Maul— including Beastly's Bargain Basement, a shop where fashion went to die—they headed

over to the Coffin Bean. And before they had even opened the coffee shop's front doors, they noted the sweet scent of rose perfume. It could mean only one thing—or, rather, one person.

Holding court inside the Gothic-style coffee shop, amid a sea of students, was none other than Miss Flapper. Instantly spotting the threesome, the delicate woman lifted herself off a small, black velvet chair and skipped over to greet them.

"Hello, and welcome to my lair," Miss Flapper cooed.

"And to think, I thought this was a coffee shop," Venus joked.

"Oh, it is. But wild dragons live in lairs, so I like to think of every room I'm in as a lair. It's rather sad how few free-roaming dragons remain in the world, and those that do tend to live in very unmonsterable climates, such as Los Fangeles and Batlanta."

"It's true," Rochelle asserted. "Monsters are predisposed to car sickness and, therefore, not well suited for driving-heavy cities."

"Have you come to join MALL?" Miss Flapper said as she leaned in to whisper in Robecca's ear.

"Deary me, I've never been very fond of whispering. It tends to tickle my ear. Plus, my father always said that people only whisper what they shouldn't be saying in the first place," Robecca said before pulling away, leaving Miss Flapper quite shocked.

"Not that Robecca thinks you're doing that," Venus attempted to explain. "Hey, look! There's Frankie Stein. We should probably go talk to her now, or we'll miss dinner."

"Of course, but please don't forget to join MALL. We need you," Miss Flapper hissed quietly before staring intently into the eyes of each girl.

"I've always loved joining clubs—although, in

126

truth, they're usually book clubs. What exactly does MALL do?" Robecca asked earnestly.

"We help monsters find their rightful place in the normie world," Miss Flapper stated solemnly.

"Please excuse us, madame, but we are on a most important mission," Rochelle explained, pulling Robecca away.

The trio headed straight for Frankie Stein as Miss Flapper watched their every move.

CHAPTER
ten

tucked away in the corner of the coffee shop, just behind Three-Headed Freddie, was the delightfully green Frankie Stein. Instead of sporting her usual warm smile, though, the girl appeared quite serious—almost forlorn, even. This marked change in expression did little to ease Rochelle's nerves about requesting a favor.

"*Pardonnez-moi*, Frankie. I am most sorry to impose upon your time, especially when you are . . . uh, actually, what is it exactly that everyone is doing here?"

"We're soaking up Miss Flapper's aura, of

129

course," Frankie said flatly, as if it were the most obvious answer in the world.

"Oh, well, I certainly do not wish to interrupt, but I was wondering if I might ask you something."

"Miss Flapper says one monster's question is another monster's answer," Frankie stated robotically, as though reciting a line from a script.

"I do not wish to bore you with the intricacies of the Gargoyle Code of Ethics, but we do not believe in asking for favors unless absolutely necessary. Therefore, with that in mind, I present myself today having already attempted and failed at this request with my own two hands," Rochelle stated seriously, greatly amusing both Venus and Robecca.

"Robecca, take it down a notch," Venus murmured quietly. "She's going to think you're asking for a kidney."

"But gargoyles do not have kidneys," Rochelle corrected Venus.

"I think what Venus meant is that this doesn't have to be such a formal affair," Robecca said with a giggle.

Rochelle then quickly returned her gaze to the green girl. "Frankie Stein, I shall now get to the point. I need your help sewing something. You see, I have these sharp claws that snag everything I touch. And as you know, it's awfully arduous to sew without touching the fabric."

"Miss Flapper says there is no greater mission than helping monsters get ahead, especially in this world that caters so much to normies," Frankie declared mechanically.

"Does that mean you'll do it?" Venus interrupted, clearly bewildered by the girl's strange behavior.

"Of course I will. What do you need sewn?"

"Can you keep a secret?" Rochelle asked seriously.

"Miss Flapper says one monster's secret is every monster's secret."

"Who knew Miss Flapper was so quotable?" Venus mumbled to Robecca.

"It's a new suit for Monsieur D'eath. I'm hoping that after a few renovations to his exterior, I might be able to find him a date. The man is desperately in need of some happiness."

"That certainly is kind of you," Frankie replied in a flat, emotionless tone. "And as this is a special occasion, I shall enlist the help of Clawdeen Wolf. She is, after all, a very talented designer."

"That would be *fangtastique!*" Rochelle exclaimed, clasping her stone hands together excitedly.

Back on campus and en route to dinner, Rochelle and her roommates stopped quickly at the post room, where each checked her mini crypt-box for mail. Much to Venus's delight, she already had a stack of letters from her younger brothers, all faithfully written on recycled paper. Ever the helpful friend, Robecca steamed open Venus's letters as Rochelle noted her own empty crypt. She had yet to receive even one letter from Garrott. She wondered if perhaps he had fallen for a new gargoyle, one with a more delicate touch. And though devastated at the mere idea of losing Garrott, his lack of correspondence also eased her burgeoning guilt over her crush on Deuce. Ever since she had seen the boy's eyes, she simply couldn't stop thinking about him!

133

At Rochelle's insistence, the threesome joined Mr. D'eath, the on-call faculty member, for dinner in the Creepateria. Over mashed potatoes and formaldehyde gravy, Rochelle, Robecca, and Venus desperately tried to engage their morose teacher in small talk.

"Monsieur D'eath, where do you originate from?" Rochelle asked between bites.

"The land of gray clouds and black souls," he warbled, looking down at his food despondently.

"Sounds like a real hot spot," Venus replied drily.

"How long have you been at Monster High?" Robecca piped up.

"Who knows? I can't even remember how long I've been dead," Mr. D'eath moaned before looking down at Rochelle's food. "Aren't you going to finish your formaldehyde gravy?"

"I haven't a taste or need for formaldehyde, seeing as I'm crafted from stone."

"Must be nice to be made of stone. Bones can be rather brittle and easy to break," Mr. D'eath replied with an epic sigh.

The following day, at Frankie's request, Venus, Robecca, and Rochelle headed to Miss Flapper's classroom at lunchtime. Small golden cages, each containing a miniature dragon or lizard, lined the walls of the room. Dragon whispering was an ancient technique based on the idea that by reaching a certain octave, one could hypnotize a dragon into submission. But because it was rather dangerous, teachers often started students on lizards to minimize the risk of crispy skin spots or fried fur.

135

"Well, at least the trolls are good with *someone*," Venus said as she watched two greasy beasts brush a miniature dragon's teeth. Fire-breathing often left the mouth covered in a smoky residue.

"I still cannot believe Clawdeen and Frankie finished the suit in twenty-four hours," Rochelle said, genuinely impressed.

"Especially since it took you almost forty-eight hours just to destroy the fabric," Robecca said before realizing how her comment sounded. "Wait, that didn't come out right."

"Boo la la! It's creeperific!" Rochelle squealed when she saw Clawdeen and Frankie approaching with their creation, a stunning goblin-green suit with silver stitches.

"That is seriously fang-tastic," Venus seconded as Frankie and Clawdeen held up the beautiful garment.

"*Merci boo-coup!* It's perfect," Rochelle gushed,

136

clapping her hands in delight. And though she longed to run her thin gray fingers against the suit and feel the fabric, she didn't dare—not after what had happened last time.

"Miss Flapper says the beauty of the suit lies in our own beauty. That is our talent," Clawdeen pronounced in a startlingly serious and monotone manner.

"Have you had a chance to join MALL yet?" Frankie demanded bluntly.

"No, but we plan to this afternoon," Venus

poorly covered. "We've just been so caught up with this Mr. D'eath thing and schoolwork that we haven't had time."

"Miss Flapper has an idea regarding your Mr. D'eath thing," Frankie stated while staring Rochelle directly in the eye. "She would like us to arrange a date for the two of them."

"No offense to Rochelle's pet project, but Miss Flapper is very pretty," Venus said candidly. "She'd really want to go on a date with a bony guy suffering from depression?"

"Miss Flapper says that one is always to start with a monster's heart," Clawdeen asserted authoritatively.

"She must keep you guys really busy memorizing everything she says," Venus grumbled sarcastically.

Just then Miss Flapper swept into the room, bringing with her an intoxicating wave of rose perfume. "Hello again," she said smoothly. "Have the ghouls told you of my idea?"

"Yes, they did. And I must say, I'm most thrilled," Rochelle exclaimed. "A date is just what Monsieur D'eath needs!"

"But what about you? What do you need, Rochelle?" Miss Flapper asked as she leaned in, bringing her pristine features into sharper focus.

"I do not need anything, Miss Flapper, but thank you for asking."

"The world is not built for us; it's built for the normies. That is why I do hope you'll join MALL soon."

"I don't know if we're MALL material. I mean, we can barely get our homework done and keep track of our pets," Venus joked.

"A monster cannot conquer the world without other monsters' support."

"True, but that's why I have these two," Venus said uncomfortably while pointing to Rochelle and Robecca.

Miss Flapper stared coldly at Venus, her intensity increasing exponentially by the second.

"What pretty earrings you are wearing. Might I take a closer look?" Miss Flapper asked Venus, prompting the girl's leaves to stand on end, though she couldn't say why.

"Um, of course. But they're not very special. They are not even real gold. Actually, they might even be plastic."

As Miss Flapper leaned closer, all the while maintaining eye contact with Venus, a sudden burst of wetness washed over the room. Headmistress Bloodgood, accompanied by Miss Sue Nami, was fast approaching.

"Miss Flapper, I am terribly sorry for my absence yesterday, but, you see, I left my head

140

in the maze, and it took Miss Sue Nami ages to find it."

While the headmistress spoke, Venus, Rochelle, and Robecca quickly slipped out of the room, leaving Miss Flapper visibly displeased.

CHAPTER eleven

D r. Clamdestine was an odd man; there was simply no way around that. After all, he had once pretended to smoke a pipe made of cheese. But on this particular day, the man was downright bizarre.

"Effective immediately, we are no longer reading *The Wonderful Wizard of Clawz*. It has come to my attention that the book carries subliminal anti-monster messages, which I refuse to condone or propagate. Instead, we shall now read *Normie Versus Monster*, one of the most important books ever written on monster oppression," Dr.

Clamdestine stated in an uncharacteristically flat and emotionless voice.

"*Pardonnez-moi*, but *Normie Versus Monster* is not even on the syllabus. I should know, as I carry a laminated copy of it with me at all times," Rochelle explained seriously.

"In order for the future generation of monsters to be successful, they must know the struggles of the past generation."

"Who said that?" Venus asked. "Lord Siren?"

"No, those wise words came from our very own Sylphia Flapper," Dr. Clamdestine replied in a detached manner.

"Ugh, not you too," Venus muttered under her breath.

"Miss Flapper sure is aces," Lagoona Blue added as Dr. Clamdestine began passing out the new books.

"I hope Jackson Jekyll doesn't hear about our

reading material," groaned Venus. "He's a normie, isn't he?"

Robecca shook her head in dismay as she took one of the new books.

As soon as the bell rang, Rochelle grabbed her bag and darted for the door. Ever the overachiever, the young gargoyle was hoping to find a quiet corner to get ahead in *Normie Versus Monster* during Study Howl.

"Hey, wait," Deuce exclaimed as Rochelle dashed out of the Libury.

Upon hearing the boy's voice, Rochelle instantly froze. And though she thought it likely he was talking to someone else, she couldn't help turning around. Dressed in faded blue jeans and a black T-shirt, he looked effortlessly cool.

"Deuce," Rochelle uttered quietly, her stomach trembling with butterflies. She hadn't experienced such a feeling since the early days

145

of her courtship with Garrott.

"Do you have a minute? I kind of need to talk to someone," Deuce said while anxiously looking around for any sign of Cleo.

"Of course," Rochelle said swooningly, her gray cheeks flushed.

"But not here. It's kind of a delicate matter."

"I feel I should remind you that gargoyles are prone to breaking delicate items. So if this is regarding something glass or ceramic, I suggest you ask someone else."

"Not that kind of delicate," he said with a laugh. "Come on. Follow me before Cleo sees us."

Rochelle's stone heart nearly leaped out of her chest at the thought of being alone with Deuce. She knew she shouldn't be excited, but she simply couldn't stop herself. As she followed him, her hard little feet transformed into light fluffy clouds floating across the floor. Why, she was almost dancing by the time they sat down at the fluorescent-pink skull-shaped table in the Study Howl!

"I always forget how nice it is to actually look someone in the eyes," Deuce said as he removed his sunglasses, showcasing his beautiful face.

"Yes, I agree," Rochelle gushed. "So, what is it you wanted to talk to me about? Do you and Cleo need help mounting a Scream Queen and King campaign for the Dance of the Delightfully Dead? I'm sure you guys will win; you are the incumbents, after all. I'm sorry—I'm rambling. What did you say you wanted to discuss?"

"Did you happen to see Spectra's article in the *Gory Gazette* today?"

"About the winds of change blowing through Monster High? I must say, it was a bit too poetic for my own journalistic preferences, but yes, I did read it."

"She wrote something about how the students' personalities were shifting and growing, and, well, it got me thinking. Something has felt off at Monster High lately. At first I thought it was just Cleo; she's become really distant and preoccupied—and not with fashion or hair. Actually, she doesn't even care about what she wears anymore, which totally blows my mind. But then I noticed other people acting weird too. And their voices—it's like they've all gone flat, almost robotic. I know it sounds silly, but I can feel it in my gut. Something's up. Anyway, I was wondering if you had noticed anything."

"Can I ask why you came to me with this concern? After all, you hardly know me."

"Gargoyles are straight shooters. You say things exactly as they are. That quality isn't easy to find, trust me." Deuce looked directly at her. "So, have you noticed anything?"

"Besides your amazing green eyes?" Rochelle babbled before getting hold of herself. "I suppose people *are* acting weird, but we're monsters. . . . Don't we always act weird?"

"Wise words, gargoyle, wise words."

Rochelle couldn't help but blush upon hearing Deuce call her "gargoyle" in such a friendly manner. It felt like a nickname or an inside joke, proof of a connection, however tenuous, between the two of them. All the way back to the dorm, she replayed continuously in her mind the sound of him saying "gargoyle." And though she was only remembering what it had sounded like, her cold granite skin warmed each time she heard it.

With Deuce dominating her every thought, Garrott could not have seemed farther away. But then Rochelle spotted a zombie in the dormitory corridor, waiting just outside the Chamber of Gore and Lore. And it wasn't just any old zombie; it was a DeadEx delivery zombie! And there was only one thing to deduce: Garrott must have sent her something! The wave of guilt she felt was sudden and stifling, squeezing every last drop of air from her lungs until she was sure they would simply crumble to dust.

"Grrrlllll Stllll?" the zombie muttered incoherently.

"Yes, that's me," Rochelle said with a guilty gulp as she signed for the package, having recognized Garrott's beautiful penmanship.

Overwhelmed with emotion and unable to face her roommates, Rochelle rushed down the hall to the sitting room and promptly collapsed into a puddle of tears. When a gargoyle cries, the tears simply drip off, literally pooling around the feet. And while this manner of crying protected the granite from unnecessary erosion, it could also make quite a mess.

In an effort not to flood the room, Rochelle held her head out the window as she cried. It wasn't the most comfortable stance while shedding tears, but it was far less messy than crying inside. Ever the levelheaded gargoyle, she thought of such things even in the midst of an emotional crisis. And though Rochelle considered her decision to hang out the window rational, Venus was more than a little shocked to find her roommate in such a peculiar position.

"I am going to take this as a sign that you've been spending too much time with Mr. D'eath," Venus announced, yanking Rochelle back into the room.

"I wasn't going to jump," Rochelle explained through sniffles. "I just didn't want to make a mess."

"While I commend your environmentally friendly repurposing of tears, I don't think it's very prudent for a creature crafted from solid stone to hang out a window," Venus said while patting a nearby chair. "Now, sit down and tell me what's the matter."

"Not to worry, I could never have fallen out," Rochelle commented as she climbed atop a chair upholstered in mummy gauze. "Venus! Oh, Venus! I don't wish to impose my problems on you."

"We're friends now, and that's what friends do. So, come on, spill it."

"I'm a terrible gargoyle! I should be thrown out of the gargoyle association and ground up into gravel!" Rochelle wailed.

"While I totally accept that there might be a gargoyle association—since you guys love rules, whether it's talking about them or making them up—there is no way they would ever gravel-ify you," Venus assured her. "Now, out with it. What happened?"

"Garrott sent me a DeadEx!" she managed to squeeze out before once again dissolving into a fit of tears.

"Was it a letter or a card? Were you disappointed he didn't just e-mail it to you and skip the hefty zombie carbon footprint?" Venus said. "Wait, I think I'm getting a little off topic. What was in the DeadEx?"

"I don't know. I haven't opened it! I feel too guilty! Garrott is sending me packages from Scaris, and what am I doing? Daydreaming about Deuce!"

Venus grabbed the large envelope and ripped it open in one fell swoop. She pulled out a single sheet of pink paper and read it slowly to herself. "What do you want first: the good news or the bad news?" she asked Rochelle.

"Excuse me?"

"Okay, let's start with the bad news. It's better

153

to end on a high note," Venus said before clearing her throat theatrically. "It's a love poem."

Rochelle shook her head, utterly racked with guilt.

"But the good news is, it's not a very good one."

"Why is that good news?" Rochelle wondered aloud.

"Hello? Because it shows that neither one of

you is perfect. You may have an itty-bitty crush on Deuce—along with half the other ghouls at Monster High—but Garrott writes really boring and derivative love poems," Venus said, walking away with the note.

"Wait! What are you doing?"

"Putting it in the recycling bin."

"But it's a love poem from Garrott!" Rochelle protested.

"So you're saying you want to keep it?" Venus asked, dangling the paper in the air.

"Yes," Rochelle replied emphatically.

"Okay, fine," Venus relented. "But promise me that if you guys ever break up, you'll recycle that piece of paper."

Rochelle nodded her head, oddly comforted by Venus's peculiar words. Perhaps her pollen-potent friend was right; maybe everyone was imperfect, including Garrott. She then recalled the many times he had lost his temper after pigeons mistook him for a statue. Garrott's intense anti-pigeon stance had caused bouts of bickering between the two of them. Rochelle found his arguing with birds very unbecoming to a gargoyle. Although the same could certainly be said for crushing on someone while engaged in a relationship with someone else. But she kept reminding herself that she had not betrayed any of the numerous gargoyle oaths she had taken. (Rather unsurprisingly, gargoyles were very fond of both writing down their rules and reciting them.)

"Rochelle, wipe up your tears. Everything is going to be just fine," Venus said sweetly.

"Thank you." Rochelle smiled, genuinely touched by her friend's helpfulness.

"I'm serious, though. You need to wipe up your tears, or we'll get in trouble for messing up the common room," Venus explained.

"Of course," Rochelle said meekly before perking up. "We should probably go find Robecca. I know she'd be disappointed if she missed sending Mr. D'eath off on his first date in the afterlife."

"Totally. I'll check the room for her and then meet you at Mr. D'eath's office," Venus agreed. "I still can't believe Miss Flapper wants to go on a date with him. She is way out of his league, but then again, she's also super creepy!"

CHAPTER twelve

Standing in the doorway of her room, Venus let out an ear-piercing screech. "*What* is going on? This is definitely not acceptable behavior!"

"Vhy are you yelling?" Blanche Van Sangre said, stifling a yawn.

"Gee, I don't know. Maybe because you and your weird sister are sleeping in my bed!"

"Vhat? Ve are gypsies. Ve don't like to stay in the same place more than a few nights," Rose explained while slowly peeling herself from the covers.

"Plus, it's not like you vere using the bed at the moment," Blanche added as she slipped on her black velvet cape.

"That doesn't mean it's okay for you to use it as some sort of gypsy-vampire day care where you come to take naps!"

"Fine, next time ve vill sleep in Rochelle's bed," Blanche said indignantly.

"In case I haven't made myself clear, there's not going to be a next time. Now, will you guys get out of here? I have somewhere I need to be," Venus grumbled while shooing them out of the room.

"*If we put monsters first, the world will no longer be cursed,*" the twins sang quietly as they flounced out the door with Venus directly behind them.

160

"Mr. D'eath!" Robecca howled with delight. "You look even better than the bee's knees!"

"I have to agree. You look pretty sharp," Venus said before winking at the still gloomy-faced man; after all, a suit can only change so much.

"You look like a fine middle-aged monster," Rochelle said in her usual blunt manner. "And remember you must compliment Miss Flapper on her appearance, pull out her chair, and, above all else, do not tell her about your regret list! Unless, of course, you want to add this date to the list."

"Yes, yes, I understand," Mr. D'eath mumbled before releasing his trademark sigh.

"And maybe try not to sigh *quite* so much," Venus added.

Robecca shook her head.

"What? Not everyone digs the sigh. It was just a suggestion."

"*Bonsoir et bon chance*, Monsieur D'eath," Rochelle said, squeezing his arm sweetly.

"Ouch!" Mr. D'eath squeaked before shooting the gray girl an annoyed look.

"Sorry," Rochelle said, embarrassed. "Sometimes I don't realize my own strength."

After escorting Mr. D'eath to Miss Flapper's classroom, the girls headed back toward the dormitory. However, they had made it only halfway through the main corridor when Venus noticed the troll with the red nose staring at her intently, his eyes bulging with nervous energy. As the creature motioned for her to follow him, Venus immediately felt ill at ease, unsure what to do. Although she was tempted to ignore the unattractive little beast, her curiosity got the better of her. Simply put, she wanted to know what the little thing was trying to tell her, even if it was absolute rubbish.

"Hey, I'll meet you guys upstairs. I forgot my Mad Science book in the lab," she said to her roomies.

"You are welcome to share mine," Robecca offered kindly.

"Thanks, but I wasn't socialized properly as a seedling, so sharing isn't really my strong suit," Venus fibbed awkwardly before ducking around the corner.

Standing in front of a row of pink coffin-shaped lockers next to the Absolutely Deranged Scientist Laboratory was the small and grubby red-nosed creature.

"I warn you! Now too late!" he muttered, his eyes darting anxiously around the purple-floored corridor.

"Warned me about what?" she asked.

"You no listen! Now too late. School dead," he grunted fearfully.

"I still don't understand. Can you please explain it to me again?" Venus pleaded.

"Too late," the troll grumbled before wobbling off at record speed, an act that greatly belied his stocky frame and advanced age.

"Wait! Wait," Venus said, running after him.

"Monster Advancement League League! Miss Snapper!" he hissed.

"You mean Miss Flapper? The dragon whisperer?"

"No dragon whisperer. *Monster* whisperer," the troll said with terror emanating from every pore. "She have all trolls but me. Soon she have all of you," he pronounced grimly, then scurried away.

Venus walked back to the dorm, her brain working overtime to comprehend what she had just heard. As she nervously twisted a vine around

164

her finger, she went over the troll's words in her head. The truth had finally been revealed. Miss Flapper wasn't a dragon whisperer; she was a *monster* whisperer. It all suddenly seemed so obvious. She hadn't any of the burns or marks associated with dragon whispering. Plus, everyone around her seemed to be under an impenetrable spell. Friendly students such as Frankie Stein were now cold, lacking in social skills, and completely obsessed with Miss Flapper.

This begged one question: What was Miss Flapper after? What did she seek to gain from controlling Monster High?

While Venus was making her way to the dorm, Robecca took Penny down to the maze for a spin, a feeble attempt to cheer up her grumpy pet penguin. Apparently, Chewlian had bitten Penny's wing earlier in the day after mistaking it for a cookie. But Robecca's best efforts came to a rather disappointing end when she promptly misplaced Penny in the maze.

"Deary me! Penny is going to kill me," Robecca moaned, steam pouring out of her ears as she began a frantic search for her friend. After flipping on her rocket boots and performing an aerial sweep of the maze, Robecca returned to the ground, unsure where to look next.

"Hi, Robecca," Cy Clops said softly as he emerged from the shadows with Penny in hand. "I hope I didn't scare you."

"You found Penny! Thank you! Jeez Louise, you really are the most helpful boy on campus!"

"I don't know about that. . . ."

"No, it's true. Whether I'm asking for the time or looking for my penguin, you always seem to be there, ready to help."

Cy looked up at Robecca with his large green eye and smiled. She was suddenly struck by what an innocent and compassionate face the boy

167

had. He seemed entirely incapable of anything dubious or underhanded.

"I'm glad I've been able to help you," he said before breaking into a shy smile.

"Do you mind if I ask—are you helping others on campus as well?" she inquired.

"No, just you." He blushed.

"Does that mean you've been following me on purpose?"

"I just wanted to make sure you were safe." Cy swallowed audibly, clearly overwhelmed by conversing with Robecca. After months of imagining such a moment, having it transpire felt downright surreal. Plus, she was even more beautiful up close than he had ever thought possible. And though she often sported frizzy hair and a steam-drenched face, he considered her absolutely perfect.

"At first I just thought you were pretty, and

168

I liked looking at you. But as time passed and things around here started getting stranger, I guess I wanted to protect you. To be there in case anything happened."

"But what could happen?" she wondered. "We're at school."

"Something isn't right at Monster High," Cy said quietly, looking around to make sure they were alone.

"You mean the food? I admit, it's not the best I've had, but what can we expect? It's Creepateria food."

"Not the food. Actually, I don't mind what they serve here; it's a lot better than what my mom makes at home," Cy said with a slight grin. "I was referring to the meetings."

"What meetings?"

"The MALL meetings. Miss Flapper holds them in the dungeon."

"School clubs are hardly illegal!" Robecca laughed.

"One day I forgot my bag after detention . . ."

"You had detention?" Robecca asked with genuine surprise.

"I fell a little behind in my homework while following you around. Anyway, I went back to the dungeon to find my book and . . ." Cy trailed off.

"Good golly, Miss Molly! Don't leave me hanging! What did you see?"

"A room full of people whispering to one another. It was like a thousand snakes hissing at once! I know it sounds ridiculous, but if you had seen it, you would have gotten the—"

"Heebie-jeebies?" Robecca interjected.

"I was going to say 'creeps,' but that works too."

"To tell you the truth, I've never liked whispering," Robecca explained as she racked

170

her brain for a logical explanation for what Cy had described.

"My mother always says that if you have to whisper it, you probably shouldn't be saying it," Cy offered.

"Exactly!" Robecca responded emphatically.

"Might I walk you home now?" Cy asked shyly. "I should probably check on Henry."

CHAPTER
thirteen

onsicur D'eath, there you are! I have been looking for you for *days*," Rochelle called out dramatically as she entered the Libury.

"Why were you looking for me?" Mr. D'eath asked, crossing his arms and narrowing his bloodshot eyes at Rochelle.

"I wanted to check in and see how your date with Miss Flapper went."

"She is going to save us all, keep us on the straight and narrow, and make sure we reach our destiny," Mr. D'eath said mechanically.

"*Pardonnez-moi*, but I am a bit confused. You are speaking of Miss Flapper like she is your life coach, not your ghoulfriend. What happened?"

"Is that some sort of dig? A dead man with a life coach?" Mr. D'eath snapped.

"Not at all. I just meant that Miss Flapper doesn't sound like your date so much as your guru."

"Do not find fault with the Flap," Mr. D'eath admonished coldly.

"The Flap? Is that your nickname for her?" Rochelle asked, confused.

"That is how she is now formally referred to at Monster High," he announced. "Anyone speaking ill of her or calling her by her former name shall be met with detention."

"I'm sorry. I wasn't aware of the name change or the policy change regarding free speech," Rochelle huffed.

174

"The Flap had a feeling you were trying to undermine her, to turn us against her work," Mr. D'eath continued, his eyes growing wide with paranoia.

"Monsieur D'eath, I haven't a clue what you are talking about."

"She said you'd say that," Mr. D'eath grumbled before releasing his trademark sigh.

"I think I'd best be going." Rochelle turned toward the door.

"Not too far now. The Flap is going to want to talk to you and your friends," Mr. D'eath said calmly, sending a chill up Rochelle's stony spine.

Feeling both unnerved and hurt by Mr. D'eath's behavior, Rochelle quickly exited the Libury and darted into the corridor. As she hurried back to the dormitory and the comfort of her room, she felt the familiar tickle of tears in her eyes. It wasn't so much what Mr. D'eath had said

175

that upset Rochelle; it was the manner in which he had said it. There was a distinct lack of personality in his voice, something she had never heard before.

"Though I lack a medical degree, I believe my diagnosis to be accurate. Monsieur D'eath has gone mad! *Complètement fou!* He's lost all touch with reality. And perhaps worst of all, he seems very ill-tempered!" the normally rational Rochelle cried upon bursting into the Chamber of Gore and Lore.

"Forget about Mr. D'eath!" Robecca replied hysterically. "Miss Flapper is holding strange whispering sessions at her MALL meetings. They hiss at one another like snakes! What in the name of the flea's sneeze do you make of that?"

"I'd say we're dealing with a monster whisperer," Venus stated firmly as she entered the room, carefully locking the door behind her.

"A monster whisperer! What does that even mean?" Robecca squealed.

"It means Miss Flapper's able to use her voice to hypnotize monsters," Venus explained.

"But why would she want to do such a thing?" Rochelle gasped. "Monsieur D'eath! Ah! She must have gotten to him already!"

"What in the foul owl are we going to do?" Robecca asked nervously.

"Robecca, there is no need to grind your gears! All we need to do is notify Headmistress Bloodgood of the situation, and she'll take care of everything," Rochelle stated calmly, trying her best to ease Robecca's frazzled nerves.

"But can the headmistress handle a situation like this? She's so scattered right now. And yes, I

177

realize that I'm the pot calling the kettle black," Robecca exclaimed.

"You're right—Headmistress Bloodgood is too spaced out," Venus declared. "We'll go straight to Miss Sue Nami instead. She's rude and pushy, but she gets things done."

"The sooner we act, the better. The situation is already seriously out of control," Rochelle added, nervously tapping her fingers against Roux's back.

"Okay, let's do this! We've got a damp woman to find," Venus said as she threw open the door.

After checking in the main office, the three-some headed straight to the graveyard, having heard that Miss Sue Nami was investigating a possible gardening infraction. The planting of unregulated greenery was a serious offense, as the cross-pollination of the wrong plants could have dire consequences. As they turned the corner to

the graveyard, they were met with a most frightening scene just beyond the cemetery's spindly metal gate. Miss Flapper, dressed in a lush, red velvet dress, was engaged in hushed conversation with a student. However, this was not just any student: It was Deuce Gorgon.

Rochelle instantly gasped, throwing her small stony hands over her mouth.

"In the name of the bee's bonnet, what do we do?" Robecca mumbled, looking to Venus for a plan.

"Nothing," the vine-draped girl replied as she watched Miss Flapper's perfect pout pressed close to Deuce's ear. "It's too late."

Deuce's face went blank before morphing back to normal, just as the other students' faces had earlier, in the school's main corridor.

"Deuce!" Rochelle called out in a futile attempt to override Miss Flapper's voice.

Unfortunately, all Rochelle managed to do was attract the attention of the deranged teacher. Her face ablaze with wild excitement, Miss Flapper charged straight for the trio.

"Ghouls! I must speak with you!" the stylish dragon called out. Venus, Robecca, and Rochelle

180

exchanged tense looks before turning and racing away.

After rounding two corners and dashing across the courtyard, they were stopped in their tracks by a hoarse voice.

"Becca? Benus? Bochelle?" a troll grunted with a rather pronounced lisp.

"How do you know our names?" Rochelle questioned the troll, her stone heart pounding nervously.

Venus snorted. "Well, they aren't exactly our names, unless you've changed yours to Bochelle."

"Venus, now is not the time for humor!" Rochelle snapped.

"The Flap want see you now!" the troll barked, spraying all three with thick balls of spittle.

Venus slowly stepped away from the grotesque little creature. "I'm sorry, but we don't speak Trollish."

"No leave! The Flap see you now!" the troll screamed louder.

"*Pardonnez-moi?* Monsieur Troll, I am so sorry, but my English is not very good," Rochelle said as she and Robecca quickly followed a fast-retreating Venus.

"No run! Stop!"

"We need to get out of here! Now!" Venus hollered as the three girls broke into an all-out sprint.

And though Rochelle's stone legs moved more slowly than the others', she was still far faster than the pigeon-toed troll. In fact, so slow was the oily little creature that he couldn't even pass the rogue bullfrog bouncing next to him down the hall. This was, of course, a disheartening situation for the troll, one that he would keep to himself for fear of ridicule.

"Deary me! I don't think I can handle any more

excitement! I might blow a gasket!" Robecca blurted out as steam exploded from both her ears.

"Cool your gaskets! I hear the sound of sloshing," Venus said triumphantly. "Miss Sue Nami!" she cried upon spotting the thick, damp wall of a woman. "We need to speak with you! It's an emergency."

"You have thirty seconds, nonadult entity. I am in the middle of a plant crisis in the graveyard."

"Miss Flapper has put the campus under a spell! We're not sure why, but she's definitely done it!" Robecca explained, steam dripping from her metal forehead.

"That is the craziest thing I have ever heard," Miss Sue Nami barked incredulously.

"I know, but it's true," Rochelle pleaded with the stern-faced woman.

"I never said it wasn't true. I just said it was the craziest thing I had ever heard," Miss Sue Nami retorted in her usual no-nonsense manner. "I must admit, I've had suspicions about Miss Flapper since day one! I don't trust popular people. I never have, and I never will."

"Thank heavens for your unhappy school years," Venus mumbled to herself.

"You needn't worry. I am going to handle this situation immediately," Miss Sue Nami said confidently. "Might I suggest you go to your room and stay out of the fray?"

"I think that is a very sound idea," Rochelle immediately piped up.

"I should have known something like this would happen. What kind of a self-respecting teacher gives herself a nickname?" And with that, Miss Sue Nami marched off, her feet pounding loudly against the ground.

CHAPTER
fourteen

no sooner had the threesome returned to the Chamber of Gore and Lore than they heard a light, almost inaudible knock at the door.

"I swear, if that's the twins coming back for another nap, I am going to go mental on them!" Venus announced as she stood to get the door.

"What if it's a troll?" Robecca inquired anxiously. "Sent to drag us back to Miss Flapper's heavily perfumed lair?"

"Who is it?" Venus grunted aggressively through the door.

"It's Cy Clops. You may not remember me, but I'm in a few of your classes. I'm the guy with one big eye. I live in the dorm with Henry Hunchback," Cy babbled as Venus opened the door in a fit of giggles.

"We know who you are, Cy," Venus said sweetly, gesturing for him to enter.

"Hi, Robecca. Hi, Rochelle." Cy awkwardly crossed his arms and looked down at the floor.

"We found Miss Sue Nami," Robecca said assuredly. "She said she's going to handle everything."

"Everything? I don't think she knows what she's up against. None of us do. I hope I'm wrong, but I don't think Miss Flapper is going to leave easily. She's got the whole school behind her now. Even Henry," Cy explained with a hint of sorrow.

"How did she get to Henry?" Rochelle asked. "The Monster Advancement League League?"

"I told Henry about what I saw in the dungeon. He went to check it out for himself, but when he returned, he wasn't the same."

"He will be again soon," Robecca said reassuringly as Cy leaned against the wall.

"Ouch!" Cy squealed before looking down to see what had bitten him.

"Sorry! I really need to put up a sign or something," Venus apologized. "'Beware—Hungry Plant on Duty.'"

Venus convinced the others that hiding out in the bell tower was far safer than staying in the room, on the off chance any trolls came looking for them. And so Venus, Rochelle, Robecca, and Cy slipped quietly into the chamber atop the tower and waited. In between stolen glances out the open windows, they played cards, napped intermittently, and speculated endlessly on what was happening outside. Occasionally the sound of trolls marching in the halls echoed up through the stone tower, but mostly there was a shroud of silence.

"I really wish we knew what was happening out there. Do you think it's possible that the power struggle is over and we're waiting up here for no reason?" Robecca inquired hopefully.

"I doubt it. Miss Sue Nami would send a signal, something to alert us," Venus hypothesized.

Small puffs of steam exited Robecca's ears. "This experience has taught me that I would not do well in jail. I'm just not wired for staying in one place. It feels unnatural."

"Unless talking about cat's pajamas or mouse's houses suddenly becomes illegal, I cannot imagine what you will ever go to jail for. Venus, on the other hand, I can imagine in jail for a wide variety of well-meaning but reckless reasons," Rochelle stated matter-of-factly.

"And what about you?" Venus shot back.

"Gargoyles are too good at following rules to wind up in jail," Cy added.

"Well put, Cyclops," Rochelle said with a smile.

Suddenly, the faint semblance of calm evaporated as a shrill and deafening ring cut through campus. The quartet exchanged tense expressions and furrowed brows as if to say *Now what?*

Voices carried up from the hall. "Emergency meeting! Emergency meeting!" "Vampitheater now! Vampitheater now!"

"What do you think?" Cy asked the group.

"It could be Miss Sue Nami holding a meeting to announce the end of Miss Flapper's reign," Venus guessed.

"Or it could be Miss Flapper herself!" Rochelle exclaimed.

"I have faith that it's Miss Sue Nami," Robecca said in an optimistic tone.

"Unfortunately, there's only one way to find out," Venus stated with palpable anxiety.

The tower stairwell was dark, damp, and desperately in need of a renovation. Splintered cracks lined the walls, and the sound of dripping water echoed ominously. It was a creepy space,

192

one that they were more than happy to escape—
at least until they saw the rampant chaos in the
hall. Students were in a literal stampede toward
the Vampitheater. And while it was hard to believe
that Miss Sue Nami would allow such disorder,
the foursome continued to hope against reason
that she was still in charge.

The purple-and-gold assembly hall was packed
to the gills, just as it had been at the start-of-the-
term assembly. This time, however, the room was
filled with mounting anxiety and tension instead
of excitement and anticipation. Robecca, Cy,
Venus, and Rochelle slipped into the last row and
quickly slouched down in their seats, all the while
keeping an eye out for trolls.

"Hello, students. I'm so happy that you all heard

the bell and were able to come," Headmistress Bloodgood stated calmly.

"She seems pretty normal, so that's a good sign," Venus muttered encouragingly to Robecca.

"As many of you know, I have waited years to ring the emergency bell!" the headmistress continued. "It's been one of my lifelong dreams to have an emergency so big that it actually warranted the bell. And I am proud to say that today I do. Now if I could only remember what it was. . . . Bat flu? Mutant insect invasion? Pumpkin-head mold virus? Or perhaps I just wanted to say hello. Oh yes, that must have been it. Hello, monsters! Thank you all for coming!"

As Headmistress Bloodgood waved to the audience, Miss Sue Nami barreled onto the stage, ramming into her boss.

"Miss Sue Nami? Are we wrestling?" Headmistress Bloodgood asked as she assumed a peculiar stance.

"Ma'am, we are most certainly not wrestling!" Miss Sue Nami barked before whispering into the headmistress's ear.

"Oh yes," Headmistress Bloodgood exclaimed. "What a relief it is to have my thoughts back! Thank you."

Watching Miss Sue Nami remind Headmistress Bloodgood of what to say greatly calmed Venus's nerves. It reminded her of her first day at Monster High, back when she thought the school seemed like a healthy place for a plant to grow. Although Venus still wasn't sure exactly what was happening, there was no denying the presence of a highly threatening epidemic.

"My young monsters, as you know, I absolutely love my job. It is most definitely the best job in the whole world. And perhaps even the most important one. Here at Monster High, we are shaping the future generation through education and preparation," the headmistress rambled excitedly.

"Is she talking about the SATs?" Rochelle muttered to herself.

"I have led you well—or at least I think I have. I can't quite remember at this exact moment. But if for some reason I haven't led you well, please keep that information to yourself. Women of my age are no longer interested in constructive criticism. What's the point? We're too old. And to that end, I feel that I am now too old to lead you in the manner you require. You need a leader who can help you take your rightful place in the world as the dominant species. No longer fourth on the list after normies, canines, and ferrets."

"Who puts us after ferrets?" Venus mumbled as her stomach twisted nervously.

196

"And so I now pass the reins of headmistress to the Flap, effective immediately."

Surrounded by trolls dressed in navy-and-red military uniforms, Miss Flapper strode up the steps to the stage. It was a shocking display of power and confidence. Gone was any semblance of the softness Miss Flapper had previously displayed. In its place was a hardness that bordered on arrogance. Dressed in a severe black dress with a high neckline, a flurry of buttons, and shoulder tassels, the outfit had a distinct military feel to it. Completing the meticulous look of power was a harsh coiffure, her red hair knotted in a tight bun atop her head.

A stern-faced Miss Flapper slowly approached the podium, dramatically drawing out each step. "Today we start again. Today we begin to build the new empire. And with that in mind, I hereby abolish all frivolous studies and irrelevant activities like Roller Maze and Fearleading. For as

197

we prepare to take our rightful place in the world, we have no time for distractions or dissension. Anyone who isn't with us is against us. There is no in-between, not anymore. We are now warriors; no longer will we be marginalized by the normies!" Miss Flapper declared before snapping her wings open for emphasis.

"What in the name of the Finnish finger did she just say?" Robecca asked Cy in a markedly panicked manner.

"I don't want to scare you, but this isn't good," he replied.

"No, this isn't even bad. This is horrible," Venus said, her face wilting with disappointment.

Miss Flapper then waved to the crowd as a chorus of uniformed pumpkin heads joined her onstage to sing the Monster Advancement Anthem.

"*If we put monsters first, the world will no longer be cursed. . . .*"

The four shell-shocked students ambled into the main corridor, unsure what their next move was, or even if they had one. With low-hanging heads and mist-filled eyes, they did not immediately notice the flyers posted all over the pink coffin-shaped lockers. But soon they spied the rather ungenerous drawings of their faces that adorned posters with the message WANTED FOR QUESTIONING— PLEASE REPORT ANY AND ALL SIGHTINGS TO THE NEAREST TROLL.

"Keep your heads down and follow me," Venus instructed the others while doing her best to avoid eye contact with anyone in the hall.

"Dear, oh, dear," Robecca whimpered. "I'm steaming! I'm steaming! I'm steaming!"

"Shh," Rochelle admonished Robecca. "Take off your sweater and wrap it around your head like a scarf. That should block at least part of it."

Cy watched Robecca closely as she wrapped her polka-dot sweater over her ears and continued down the corridor after Rochelle and Venus. He couldn't explain why he felt so protective of her, but he did. Ever since the first time he laid his eye on the metallic young lady, he had longed to be near her.

After ducking into the maze, Robecca performed an aerial sweep to find the most deserted spot in which to take refuge. Hidden amid a cluster of unkempt hedges, wayward-growing trees, and rusted old contraptions, the quartet began to absorb the severity of the situation.

"*Je ne comprends pas!* Why is Miss Flapper after us? What did we do?" Rochelle pondered aloud.

"Those posters are straight out of the Wild West," Robecca said with steam pouring directly out of her ears and onto Cy's face. "Deary me, sorry about that!"

"Actually, it feels really good. I forgot my eyedrops in the dorm."

"I just don't get it. Why us? Are we the only ones not under her spell? Or is it something else?" Venus questioned no one in particular.

"We're the only four people on campus who didn't join MALL. It's that simple. We're literally the last ones standing," Rochelle said with a glum expression reminiscent of Mr. D'eath's.

"She's right," Cy agreed. "Miss Flapper clearly knows who's in and who's out."

"Maybe we should go into town and try to talk to the sheriff," Robecca suggested.

"And say what? That the new headmistress is brainwashing everyone?" Venus replied. "I somehow doubt he'll believe us. But even if he does, and he comes here, we run the risk that the sheriff will fall under her spell too. That could prove catastrophic for Salem."

"I wish we were in Scaris! Then I would know exactly what to do. Call the gargoyle support line, report the problem, and finally wait for the committee to arrive and advise on the issue."

"We may not have an advice committee, but we have one another," Robecca muttered. "That's got to count for something."

"Cy?" Venus interrupted. "I can't stop thinking about what you said in the room—that none of us know what we're up against. You're right, and unless we do, we're never going to be able to stop her."

"I think we should begin by reviewing what we do know about Miss Flapper," Rochelle proposed.

"She transferred here from a monster academy in Bitealy," Robecca said, "and she got a bunch of elderly trolls as a parting gift."

Venus nodded. "We need to talk to people at her old school, find out why she left, find out everything they know about her."

"Then we need to break into the main office and find Miss Flapper's personnel file," Cy advised.

"Cy, I never knew you were such a rebel," Robecca cooed, clearly impressed by the boy's willingness to break the rules.

"As you know, I do not believe in or condone breaking and entering. I do, however, see that in this case it is necessary, for the greater good," Rochelle babbled.

"You don't have to come with us if it makes you uncomfortable," Venus stated. "The three of us can handle it."

"I will be there. As Robecca said, we're in this together, and that's got to count for something."

"Is that part of the Gargoyle Code?" teased Venus.

"It's part of the Rochelle Goyle code."

CHAPTER
fifteen

With their faces plastered all over the school, getting to the main office without detection was nearly impossible. And so it was decided that they would wait until nightfall before leaving the maze.

That night, under the sound of swooping bats, Robecca, Rochelle, Venus, and Cy crept slowly down the main corridor, their eyes peeled for trolls. Much had changed during the Flap's short time in power. Memos with new rules were e-mailed hourly, covering everything from the complete suppression of free speech to the trolls' revised dress code. According to the latest mandate, trolls were to wear navy-and-red suits, comb their hair into ponytails, and march in military formation whenever patrolling the halls.

"What does it say about trolls that it took all this to get them to shower?" Venus noted while the group hid in a dark doorway and waited for the last troop of trolls to retire for the night.

"It means exactly what we already knew: that they're a species that does not hold personal hygiene in high regard. It is for this reason that the *Gargoyle Traveler's Guide* warns against accepting invitations from trolls," Rochelle responded.

With the coast clear, Venus led the others past the Creepchen and the Absolutely Deranged Scientist Laboratory and finally to the large metal door of the main office.

"It's locked," Robecca whispered. "Venus, I'm

guessing you know how to pick a lock with your vines."

"What does that mean?"

"Please, move out of the way," Rochelle instructed the others. "For once my hard little claws might be of some use."

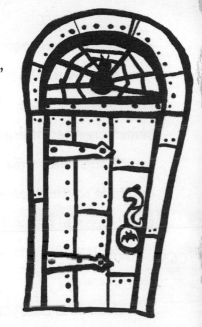

Rochelle sanded down the lock's mechanism until the door simply popped open. Once inside the crowded and messy office, the quartet split up, desperate to locate Miss Flapper's personnel file and return to the maze.

Seated on an office chair scanning papers, a thoroughly focused Rochelle didn't notice the creaking sound coming from beneath her. The chair was, in fact, calling for help, desperately pleading for someone to save it. It was a rather common occurrence for furniture to literally beg for its life while beneath the slender yet weighty creature. But alas, she was far too preoccupied searching for information on Miss Flapper to notice the chair's distress. Why, it was only upon crashing to the floor, atop a mass of broken wood, that Rochelle realized there was a problem.

"Rochelle?" a familiar voice called out from the doorway.

"Deuce? Is that you?"

"Are you okay? That looked like quite a fall," the boy said as he approached her, wearing his trademark sunglasses.

"Yes, I'm fine. Sadly, breaking chairs is not new for me," Rochelle explained, wondering whether Deuce might have miraculously escaped Miss Flapper's spell.

"Well, I'm glad you're all right," he said emotionlessly. The boy then noticeably tensed up, as if he had just remembered that he was talking to one of the school's most wanted monsters. "Rochelle, what exactly are you doing in the office?"

"I was recently appointed midnight office clerk by the Flap," Rochelle fibbed uncomfortably while covertly motioning for the others to stay hidden.

"Rochelle, that's a lie," Deuce replied firmly.

"Please, don't say anything. We're just trying to get the school back to normal."

"The Flap will want to speak with you. I have no choice but to take you to her right now."

"Please, Deuce, just let me go," Rochelle said, signaling the others to start for the door.

"I can't do that. . . ." Deuce replied slowly.

"Sure you can. It's just me, Rochelle, the one ghoul who's looked into those kind eyes of yours."

"You're betraying your own kind, and that is not right," Deuce stated resolutely. "I'm getting the trolls."

"Are you sure you want to do that?" Venus questioned the boy before releasing a potent pollen sneeze all over him.

"That was disgusting," Deuce responded angrily, wiping chunks of orange pollen from his face.

"Uh-oh, my pollens can't penetrate the spell."

"Troll!" Deuce hollered loudly.

"*C'est une catastrophe!*" Rochelle screamed as she and the others dashed out of the office and into the hall.

A slow runner, Rochelle had no hope of shaking Deuce. Except that at the exact moment he chased the gargoyle into the hall, a sea of bats flew down from the ceiling, clamoring around the boy's Mohawk of snakes. It was a well-known fact that bats and snakes had a long and bitter rivalry over the title "normies' least favorite pet." And by the time the bats had tired of taunting the snakes,

Rochelle and the others had long vanished into the night.

After safely returning to the maze, Cy revealed that he had located the name and number of Miss Flapper's former school mere seconds before Deuce's arrival in the office. In a testament to Headmistress Bloodgood's poor organizational skills, he had discovered the file beneath a potted plant.

"It's the Accademia de Mostro in northern Bitaly," Cy explained. "I'm going to need to sneak into a classroom. I need a phone with international dialing."

"Shouldn't we all go with you?" Robecca offered sweetly.

"The larger the group, the more likely we are to be noticed."

"I agree," Venus added. "But do you speak Bitealian?"

"Only what I've learned from Three-Headed

211

Freddie. I'm hoping someone at the school speaks English."

"I would try the Libury first. It's pretty close, plus I've seen Dr. Clamdestine use the phone in there many times," Rochelle said as she pressed a thin gold hatpin into his hand and whispered, *"Bon chance."*

It was nearly half past four in the morning when Cy slipped out of the maze and passed the dungeon and graveyard before coming upon the Libury door. He pulled out Rochelle's sharp and stylish hatpin and began fiddling with the lock. And although he never would have admitted it to anyone, he was quite enjoying his new life as a criminal. While unintended, the recent bout of recklessness had given him a greatly needed confidence boost.

After successfully picking the lock, Cy crept into the dusty room. On a desk in the corner, he found a well-worn black phone. After dialing a seemingly endless series of numbers, he listened to the foreign ringtone and waited.

"*Buongiorno!*" a man's voice echoed.

"Uh, *bonjeerno*," Cy replied awkwardly.

"Who is this?" the man asked in a thick Bitcalian accent.

"My name is Cy Clops, and I am a student at Monster High in Salem, Oregon, in the United States. I was wondering if I might speak to the headmistress or headmaster."

"That is me, Signore Vitriola."

"A former teacher of yours recently arrived at our school. Perhaps you remember her—Miss Flapper?"

"Yes . . ." Seniore Vitriola continued warily.

"Well, she seems to have put the school under some sort of spell, a monster whisper. . . ."

"Oh no!" the man screamed loudly. "It's spreading! Please leave me alone. Never call this number again!"

"But, sir, this is destroying our school!"

"I cannot help you. I closed the Accademia a year ago! I had no choice—I couldn't stop it."

"You mean Miss Flapper?"

"Please, I don't want to discuss this. Perhaps you will have better luck with the book than I did."

"What book?"

"You must find your school's Crybrary. . . ."

"Its what?"

"All monster academies have a secret room known as a Crybrary, where highly classified books are kept. The room is only to be accessed by someone with a master's degree in Beastly

Sciences. But I suppose in your case, an exception must be made."

"How do I find the Crybrary?"

"It's different for every school."

"Thank you, Signorc Vitriola."

"I hope, for your sake, it is not too late," the old man whispered before the line abruptly went dead.

CHAPTER
sixteen

he Crybrary did not appear on any of the
school maps, nor was there mention of it
in any report or letter. Had it not been for
the words of Signore Vitriola, they never would
have known the room existed. As they later
learned, the International Monster Federation
insisted Crybraries remain clandestine for fear of
adventurous students using the information for
less-than-appropriate endeavors.

In order to locate the elusive Crybrary, the
dormies had to unearth the original floor plans
for Monster High. Lucky for them, the blueprints

were stored in a shed hidden within the maze. After poring over the ink-stained papers, they saw one room located behind the Absolutely Deranged Scientist Laboratory that they believed was the Crybrary. However, when they went to inspect it, they found a janitor's closet.

"None of these rooms look big enough to be the Crybrary!" Venus moaned after returning to the maze to once again pore over the floor plans.

"We must keep looking," Rochelle said calmly. "We haven't any other choice."

"We could run away and join the circus," Venus joked.

"Ugh! The circus! They were after me for years," Robecca said animatedly. "But Father always said no. He thought living in a tent might lead to rust."

Cy continued studying the floor plans long after the others had fallen asleep atop nearby hedges. Though prickly, the shrubbery was surprisingly comfortable.

"Hey, ladies, I think I found something," Cy said in his usual soft manner.

The girls, who were tired both mentally and physically, did what they used to do to their parents: They rolled over and ignored him. Ever polite, Cy waited ten minutes before again trying to rouse the interest of the group.

219

"Um, I think I'm onto something. Something that will help us find the Crybrary."

"What? Why didn't you say something earlier?" Venus said, shooting straight off her shrub.

"Venus is right, Cy. You really need to learn to speak up," Robecca chided the boy as Penny shook her head at her clueless owner.

"Of course, Robecca, whatever you say."

"The anticipation is weighing very heavily on me. What is your idea?" Rochelle asked while using a bristly leaf as an exfoliant on her arm. She was always looking for new ways to soften her skin.

"Actually, I was thinking of Rochelle. . . ."

"Oh, you were, were you? Not that I blame you; she really is the bee's knees. Plus, she has that great accent. And let's be honest, everything sounds better with an accent. Deary me, what were you saying? I seem to have gone wildly off

220

course," Robecca rambled before averting her eyes in embarrassment.

"Rochelle is smaller than us, smaller than the average monster. . . ."

"While that is technically true, I am considered above average in size in the gargoyle community," Rochelle huffed.

"But she manages to retain more information than the rest of us, reciting codes and guidelines off the top of her head. . . ."

"And?" Venus pressed Cy.

"Don't you see? We all assumed that the Crybrary had to be big, and we were wrong. A small space can hold just as much information, if not more."

"Jeez Louise, Cy! You're a genius!" Robecca gushed.

"I don't know about that," he mumbled, "but I think I might have found the room. It's the smallest one on the plans."

And so the crew, dressed head to toe in black, set out from the maze in the dead of night to find the Crybrary.

"I know I shouldn't say this, but I really don't care for bats," Rochelle whispered, walking through the main corridor. "They do not appear to have a very rule-based society."

"You certainly do love your rules," Venus responded before sneaking a peek at Cy and Robecca.

"Cy, do Cyclopes ever need glasses? And if so, what do they look like? Just one big circle? Or maybe you guys prefer contact lenses? I know it's silly, but I'm terribly curious. And so is Penny. Oh dear, Penny! Wherever did I leave her? I sure hope I wound her enough," Robecca rambled.

"She's with Roux and Chewlian at the grave-yard for safekeeping, remember?"

"Oh yes, it certainly is nice to have someone around with a good memory."

"And to answer your question, Cyclopes' issues with peripheral vision and depth perception aren't really things that can be helped with glasses or contacts."

"Too bad," Robecca replied.

"Hey, guys, we're here," Cy uttered quietly, covering his face with his hands in an effort to protect his eye from an unusually low-flying bat.

The fear of getting particles, insects, or occasionally even small mammals stuck in his eye had made Cy more than a bit skittish.

"Why are we back at the laboratory?" Venus questioned.

"Follow me," the Cyclops said as he led the girls through the messy, vial-filled room and into

223

the janitor's closet.

Cy fiddled with
the sink knobs, then
the broom stand,
then the water main,
then the light
switch, but nothing happened.

"Are you sure it was behind
this room? That plan *is*
awfully hard to read," Robecca said comfortingly.

"It's here. I'm sure of it."

"Really? I'm not sure of anything anymore,"
Venus said, kicking the doorjamb with her foot.

From the ceiling came a noise similar to the
sound of a plane lowering its wheels before
landing. A thick metal ladder descended, stopping
a mere inch above the floor.

"I thought you said it was behind the room!"
Robecca exclaimed.

224

"That's what it looked like on the plan," Cy responded before grabbing on to the ladder and starting up it.

He climbed into the ceiling, then a few feet across, before lowering himself into what must have been the world's smallest library. The room was no bigger than three feet by three feet, with old leather-bound books covering every inch of the walls. Cy scanned the titles quickly (a benefit of being a Cyclops) until his eye landed on *Monster Whisperer*.

"Hey, what's going on in there?" Venus called from the janitor's closet.

"Coming," Cy responded. But when he tried to pull the volume off the shelf, he found that it was chained to the wall. He had to admit it was an effective means of preventing the usual library problems of overdue and stolen books.

After returning to the janitor's closet and

225

explaining the rudimentary security system to the girls, Cy sat back and listened as they debated how to handle the situation.

"So, who's going in there to read the book?" Robecca asked pointedly. "Obviously, I would be more than happy to, but on several occasions my roomies have alluded to my rather short attention span, so perhaps it shouldn't be me. But then again, I have always liked reading. I must have read *Alice's Adventures in Monsterland* four times when I was younger—"

"I think we can all agree that Robecca is out," Venus interrupted.

"It makes the most sense for me to go in there. I retain information better than anyone else; Cy even said as much. Plus, I am very compact and fit easily into small spaces," Rochelle posited.

"See, I was thinking I should go because I am sort of the group leader. Not to mention, I am pretty good at thinking outside the box, a skill this situation definitely calls for," Venus countered.

"I only acknowledge democratically elected leaders, and as far as I can recall, we have never held an election," Rochelle expounded seriously.

"You know, I didn't want to have to say it, but I'm afraid you'll break the ladder. Let's not forget what happened in the office. You killed a chair."

Sensing the mounting tension, Cy quickly stepped in. "What about me? Perhaps it's best I read the book. After all, I do have this really big eye."

"Fair enough," Venus relented before Rochelle nodded her head.

Cy returned ten minutes later sporting a facial expression the girls could only describe as impossible to read. Instead of immediately telling the others what he had discovered, he merely stood there, staring at the floor.

227

"Please, Cy! What in the name of the mouse's house did you find out?"

"Breaking a monster whisperer's spell is not easy," the one-eyed boy mumbled.

"Okay, we can handle *not easy*," Venus replied confidently.

"Actually it's going to be really hard," Cy continued.

"We can handle *really hard*," Venus replied assuredly.

"To be totally honest, it's near impossible," Cy admitted.

"Please, Cy, just tell us what is required," Rochelle snapped, feeling more than a bit edgy from the suspense.

"In order to break the hold, the whisperer must swallow one teaspoon of ground Fernish Bush while a recently zombified snake is wrapped around the neck."

228

"I have to admit that does sound a bit tricky," Robecca stated honestly.

"Wait, there's more," Cy said with a Mr. D'eath–worthy sigh. "It must take place at exactly midnight."

"Well, I see what you meant by *near impossible*," Venus relented. "Unfortunately, it's our only option."

Much like the bats, the foursome slept all day and worked all night in preparation for the moment of reckoning. Fortunately, some tasks proved simple, such as locating the necessary ingredients and finding a time to launch the attack on Miss Flapper. Venus happened upon both ground Fernish Bush and Burnwidth Serum in Mr. Hack's office during a midnight sleuthing mission. And as for the occasion of the attack, there was really only one option—the Dance of the Delightfully Dead. When else could they access Miss Flapper at exactly midnight? The snake, however, proved a tad bit more complicated.

"How are we going to, you know, do it?" Robecca muttered while staring at a thin gray-and-yellow snake recently removed from Miss Kindergrubber's pantry. Nonpoisonous snake-venom soup was one of the teacher's specialties.

"I don't know," Cy replied. "Mr. Hack didn't mention what to do with the serum after it was heated."

"We're just going to drop the serum into the snake's mouth until it starts looking ashen and moving slowly," Rochelle told the others.

"But how exactly are you planning on getting the snake to open its mouth?" Venus wondered. "Are you going to say 'pretty please'?"

"For your information, I thought we'd add a bit of melted cheese to the serum. Snakes, like the Scarisians, absolutely love cheese. As soon as the little thing smells the melted Camembert, he'll open up. Trust me," Rochelle huffed.

"I feel like we've all overlooked one very important matter. How are we getting into the Dance of the Delightfully Dead unnoticed?" Robecca asked. "We are, after all, wanted monsters."

"I have two words for you," Venus announced. "Drama department."

CHAPTER
seventeen

hidden between groves of tall and cumbersome pine trees was Salem's oldest and most glorious cemetery— the Skelemoanian. So grand and elaborate was the Skelemoanian that it was more than a cemetery; it was a necropolis, a city of the dead, littered with towering tombs, ornately carved mausoleums, and elaborate underground crypts. It had been built centuries earlier by Skelen Moania, an ostentatious zombie who believed that in life, death, and the afterlife, one ought never hold back. Therefore, traditional understated headstones

233

were few and far between at the Skelemoanian. Those that did exist had been worn down by years of rain and heavy foot traffic and were now mere nubs peeping through the grass.

Shrouded in shadows both day and night, the Skelemoanian was as creepy as it was spectacular. A design flaw in Skelen Moania's own family mausoleum had resulted in a faint but eerie whistle. Although it was merely the noise of wind passing through cracks in the marble structure, it sounded like someone whispering—or, when the wind was strong, wailing.

On the night of the fateful Dance of the Delightfully Dead, the wind was light, creating only the faintest hiss. So feeble was the sound that it was rather annoying, like a fly buzzing in one's ear.

The trek from campus through the dense pine forest was as uncomfortable as it was tense.

Robecca, Venus, Rochelle, and Cy not only had to navigate through branches, birds, and a wide variety of insects while dressed in werewolf costumes (lifted from the *Wolfler on the Roof* production), but they had to do so without being noticed. For if they were to be caught now, on the precipice of taking down Miss Flapper, all would truly be lost. There was no safety net to protect them or the town of Salem should they fail. Of this fact they were all painfully aware—none more so than Rochelle.

As a gargoyle, Rochelle prided herself on calm, calculated thinking that allowed her to assess every possible outcome of a scenario. This was an ability she had always relished, as she believed it kept her and those around her safe. On this night, however, Rochelle would have liked nothing more than to be lost in naive optimism, heading into battle without the consequences of failure so clear in her mind. But alas, such naïveté was impossible. Rochelle was a gargoyle, a creature burdened with both a heavy body and a heavy mind.

"Rochelle, can you try to walk a little more softly?" Venus whispered, clearly worried that the gargoyle's gait would attract attention.

"*Zut*, I am trying, but tiptoeing is not something that comes naturally to gargoyles. There is a reason we are often said to have two lead feet."

"Use your wings!"

"They make even more noise!" Rochelle hissed.

From behind Venus a large cloud of steam passed by, the product of Robecca's frazzled nerves.

"Deary me, I can't seem to calm down. I'm like a bat on a hot tin roof back here!"

"I hear singing! Quick, duck!" Venus whispered as she pulled Robecca to the ground with her.

For once, everyone was grateful for the relentless crooning of the pumpkin heads. Dressed in their finest attire, the posse of orange-headed creatures jovially made their way through the dense woods. Once the high-pitched voices had disappeared into the night, Cy started to pick himself up off the ground, but Venus grabbed his arm and shook her head. Cy didn't hear anything. As a matter of fact, no one—including Venus—heard anything. She had, however, picked up the faint smell of body odor mixed with cologne and hair product. This could mean only one thing—trolls.

Within minutes, the sound of their craggily clawed feet marching in formation could be heard and even felt. So it was hardly a surprise when a troop of ten stomped past, but it was terribly shocking to see Miss Sue Nami among them, dressed in the same navy-and-red uniform as the others. While never their friend, she had been a reliable and stable presence during their short time at Monster High, and seeing her devoid of her normal biting individuality was nothing short of disheartening.

By the time Rochelle, Venus, Robecca, and Cy had made it through the forest to the edge of the cemetery, they were all a frizzy-furred mess from both Robecca's steam and the assault of tree branches they had endured. Whatever lingering illusions they held that this undertaking would be either easy or fast dissipated at the sight of the elaborate security surrounding the Skelemoanian. So impressive was the line of defense that one might have been forgiven for thinking that Gillary Clinton or some other head of state was in attendance.

The perimeter was a literal wall of trolls, each facing outward, looking for possible agitators or enemies of the Flap.

"Heavens to Betsy!" Robecca squealed at the

sight of the trolls. "However are we going to sneak past them?"

"We're covered head to toe in werewolf fur. We're more likely to be noticed sneaking in than just walking through the main entrance," Venus assessed. "But you're going to have to do your best to control the steam, because it's pretty much a dead giveaway."

"We'd better get started," Rochelle said, pulling a small glass jar from her bag.

The thin gray-and-yellow snake slept peacefully in the container, totally unaware of the fate that awaited it.

"I must admit, I feel rather guilty zombifying this creature without its permission. I don't imagine that such behavior is condoned by the Gargoyle Code of Ethics."

"Here, hand me the vial. Cyclopes don't have a code of ethics," Cy said as he took a thin glass

239

tube filled with green fluid and small balls of Camembert cheese from Rochelle. "And the lighter?"

Cy held the flame to the glass until the cheese balls had melted and the liquid was bubbling furiously. "Let's hope this snake has a good sense of smell."

The one-eyed boy then slowly lowered a dropper into the reptile's jar. Utterly uninterested, the yellow-and-gray snake did not so much as move its head.

"It's probably lactose intolerant and hates cheese!" Venus huffed.

"No, wait! Look!" Robecca said

as the snake abruptly whipped its head back and attempted to drink from the dropper.

Having emptied the entire contents of the vial into the snake's mouth, the four students waited anxiously for any sign of zombification.

"How are we supposed to tell if it's moving slower if it's not moving at all?" Rochelle wondered rationally.

"Its skin—it's turning dull and ashen. And look at its eyes! They're all bloodshot," Cy said excitedly.

"Should we check its pulse, just to make sure?" Robecca pondered aloud.

"I don't think that's necessary," Venus declared. "It's time. We need to move."

At exactly 11:50 PM, the quartet approached the main entrance, next to which stood a large

241

limestone statue of Skelen Moania. Rather disturbingly, the sculpture was adorned in a floor-length pink Scaremès gown, a pair of delicately crafted wings, and a red wig in Miss Flapper's honor.

"What a shameful waste of couture," Rochelle grumbled as she came upon the first group of uniform-clad trolls.

"Remember, if anyone asks, we're Clawdeen's cousins from the poorly groomed side of the family," Venus muttered under her breath to the others.

The sensation of being watched weighed heavily on each of them as they passed through the channel of trolls. Venus and Rochelle were able to control their anxiety, but Cy and Robecca could not. The boy suddenly felt itchy, as if his skin were battling against the oppressive werewolf costume. And though he was able to stop himself from scratching, the suppression of the urge resulted in terrible shaking. Why, it almost appeared as though the boy were having a seizure!

Next to him, the wisps of steam exiting Robecca's nose intensified, growing stronger by the second. Unfortunately, the harder she tried to calm down, the tenser she became, in turn causing more steam to escape.

"What wrong you?" a troll grunted at a visibly shaking Cy.

"Oh, him? He's just nervous he won't be chosen Scream King because of his grubby fur," Venus joked, looping her arm through Cy's.

"What in your nose?" The troll pointed at Robecca.

"In the name of the flea's sneeze, I do believe I've ruined it all," she muttered quietly to herself as she fought the urge to cry.

"Call the Nami," the troll instructed a nearby comrade.

"No. It normal for werewolf," the other troll replied, waving them on.

When Venus looked back at him in surprise, she recognized her friend with the red nose.

The Dance of the Delightfully Dead was nothing like what they'd expected, not that any of them really knew what to expect. Instead of music and laughter, a literal wave of whispers washed over their ears. The sound was just as Cy had described it: akin to the hissing of a thousand snakes. Huddled between moss-covered mausoleums and crypts, monsters were devotedly whispering in one another's ears. The foursome wandered through the crowds, carefully avoiding eye contact for fear of being recognized.

Near the middle of the Skelemoanian, they discovered an elaborately built gold stage on which Miss Flapper stood like a queen greeting the masses. Dressed in a fabulous handcrafted black-

and-gold frock, she was undeniably beautiful.

"Time check?" Venus asked Rochelle quietly.

The gargoyle swiftly pulled out her iCoffin. "Three minutes and twenty-two seconds until midnight."

"Remember, as long as we do not diverge from the plan, we have at least a fifty percent chance of success," Venus said stoically.

"I put us closer to forty-three point five percent," Rochelle corrected her.

"Deary me, that is hardly a confidence boost!"

The four friends then patted one another on the backs and split in three different directions. Because of Robecca's notorious time issues, Cy accompanied her. Plus, he couldn't have left her side in the midst of all these monstrous maniacs.

Consumed with unbridled terror and spurred by a rush of adrenaline, the friends took their positions at the sides of the stage. At this point,

Robecca experienced a momentary understanding of time. For as she and Cy watched their iCoffins, waiting for the planned moment to strike, her mind did not wander for one second.

Rochelle was first to act, at exactly 11:59:30, climbing atop a crypt and then flinging her granite body onto the stage. As expected, this deed garnered her the attention of a nearby troll. Without a second to spare, she broke into a mad dash. Though she moved at her customary slow speed, she felt fast on her feet for the first time in her life. In reality, though, she was only an inch from being captured, when she thrust her body around Miss Flapper's feet, anchoring the teacher to the platform.

The trolls, now in a flurry, swarmed around the four friends. Venus unleashed a sneeze attack, spraying the approaching trolls with thick orange pollen. Robecca employed a similar tactic and steamed the trolls, aiming her vapors up their noses, instantly bringing them to their knees.

"It's time," Venus hollered before flinging the snake around Miss Flapper's thin ivory neck.

Robecca then quickly steamed the dainty dragon in the eye, prompting her to scream uproariously. At which point Cy simply dumped the teaspoon of ground Fernish Bush into Miss Flapper's open mouth.

"Attack! Traitors!" Miss Flapper hollered, sending Fernish Bush flying everywhere.

"No! She's losing powder," Cy screamed while Venus's tightly curled vines fought Miss Flapper's delicate but strong hands.

Rochelle held on to Miss Flapper's thin legs, her claws accidentally shredding the bottom of the deranged dragon lady's couture dress. "I feel terrible—this fabric is *fangtastique*!" Rochelle was mumbling to herself when she suddenly noticed the strange sound of silence.

All activity in the cemetery had ground to a halt, the monsters and trolls standing eerily still, almost frozen. While gazing dumbstruck at the crowd, Rochelle slowly let go of the now stationary Miss Flapper and stood up.

"*Regardez!* Everything's stopped," Rochelle quietly pointed out to the others.

"What does this mean?" Robecca whispered anxiously, steam dribbling out of both her ears.

"Maybe we did something wrong," Cy hypothesized as he surveyed the mass of motionless monsters, all sporting looks of deep confusion.

"Oh no! What did we do to them? Did we make it worse?" Venus wondered aloud, her vines quivering under the stress of the situation.

Just then a light wave of whispers began to cut through the crowd. The formerly still monsters started yawning, rubbing their eyes, and stretching.

248

"I think they're waking up!" Rochelle proclaimed excitedly.

The whispering grew loud and boisterous as the bewildered crowd roused to consciousness.

"Where am I?"

"What's happening?"

"How did I get here?"

"It worked!" Venus shouted, jumping up and down.

Not to be outdone by a bit of jumping, Robecca flipped on her boots and soared gloriously into the air. So spectacular and daring were her aerial maneuvers that the confused monsters were momentarily distracted. For a few seconds, they weren't wondering why their brains felt fuzzy; they were merely marveling at the great talent of one of their own.

"In the name of the bee's knees, I do believe we're free!" Robecca shouted joyfully before her feet once again touched the ground.

"Free from what? I don't understand what we're all doing here," Frankie Stein said, rubbing her tired green forehead.

"Hey, where's Miss Flapper? We're supposed to be on a date," Mr. D'eath groaned with understandable disappointment.

Before Robecca, Venus, or Rochelle could answer, Cleo de Nile stormed through the crowd, seething with rage. "Wait a minute! Is this the Dance of the Delightfully Dead? Why am I dressed in such a hideous outfit? Is this some kind of joke?" the Egyptian princess whined while looking down at her brown corduroy dress with a ferret's face embroidered on the front.

"Students," Headmistress Bloodgood said calmly, "let me explain."

"With all due respect, Headmistress, you can't explain. You haven't a clue what's happened here," Rochelle stated firmly.

250

"Well, I can't say that surprises me. Perhaps we should ask Miss Sue Nami instead?"

"Ma'am," the waterlogged woman barked loudly, "I am unfortunately incapable of remembering anything that has transpired. It's all fuzzy and vague, like a dream I can't quite recall."

"Well, I must say, that is a surprise!" Headmistress Bloodgood exclaimed.

"My last clear memory is of storming through the main corridor in search of Miss Flapper," Miss Sue Nami explained as she pulled at her tight military uniform.

"That's weird. The last thing I can recall is Miss Flapper too," Clawdeen muttered, inadvertently setting off a chain of Miss Flapper memories among the monsters. Soon all eyes had turned to the elegant teacher, who was still standing in the middle of the makeshift stage.

"What did you do to us?" Jackson Jekyll screamed angrily.

"This is too crazy! Ve need to take a nap," Blanche Van Sangre moaned before she and her sister slipped into a nearby crypt.

"I'm so sorry, but I haven't the faintest idea who any of you are or, for that matter, where we are," Miss Flapper murmured emotionally.

"Well, isn't that convenient?" Venus said, rolling her eyes.

Miss Sue Nami herded Sylphia Flapper, along with the rest of the students and faculty, into the Vampitheater so that Venus, Robecca, Rochelle, and Cy could explain the madness that had ensued in the prior weeks. Everyone gasped at the stories, and Miss Flapper collapsed into a heap of tears, the likes of which no one had ever seen. The dainty woman shook violently as she sobbed, clearly horrified by her actions. She claimed that she too had been under a spell that had forced her to act in such horrid ways.

Draculaura wiped away tears of empathy. "Poor Miss Flapper!"

"I know how painful it is not to be able to remember, and I can only imagine how painful it must be to not want to remember," Headmistress Bloodgood said wisely.

"Ma'am, I need to advise against fraternizing with the enemy," Miss Sue Nami stated bluntly before performing her signature shake-off all over the headmistress.

"Don't be silly, Miss Sue Nami. Miss Flapper is as much a victim as any of us. . . ."

But Robecca, Rochelle, and Venus weren't so sure; the word *victim* rang in their ears, taunting them in their uncertainty over what had transpired.

In the days that followed, Monster High fell back into its normal routine, albeit with more homework. The era of whispering had left the students behind in their studies, forcing them to learn twice as much as usual just to catch up. Dr. Clamdestine, Mr. Hack, and the other teachers even took to offering study sessions on the weekends. And following an intense debate, Headmistress Bloodgood and Miss Sue Nami decided to keep the elderly trolls on, as they were rather good at maintaining order. Plus, there was nowhere else for them to go.

In the aftermath of the disturbing occurrence, there was a sincerely heartening development: The students and faculty pulled together, determined to get their lives and their school back to normal. However, in their determination to put the whispering incident behind them, no one voiced a vital question—a question that Robecca, Venus, and Rochelle couldn't seem to get past. If Miss Flapper was, in fact, a victim like the rest of them, then who put her up to this? And, more important, why?

"I can't believe it's already time to pick our classes for next term," Robecca groaned as she climbed beneath her mummy-gauze sheets with her pet penguin.

"Robecca, you seem to have tucked the wrong end of Penny into bed," Rochelle said, pointing to the penguin's small metal feet sticking out from beneath the covers.

"Deary me!" Robecca replied with a laugh.

"So, what are you guys thinking for next term? Should we take Miss Flapper's Dragonomics class?" Venus asked the others provocatively.

"After watching our school fall under a spell and having to single-handedly rescue everyone, I am rather inclined to take it easy next term and avoid any areas of drama," Rochelle responded.

With raised eyebrows, Venus inquired, "Does that mean you're going to leave Mr. D'eath alone?"

"Of course not! I am a gargoyle; I cannot have an incomplete mission on my record! I will not rest until I see that man smile!"

"Well, thankfully, you still have a few years left at Monster High," Robecca joked.

"I don't need years; I have you guys," Rochelle said seriously. "Haven't you heard? Part of being ghoulfriends forever means we have to support one another, no matter what."

"I couldn't agree more! Ghoulfriends forever! I am absolutely thrilled to have a gargoyle as one of the founding members of Monster High's compost heap!" Venus smirked.

"Venus, *s'il ghoul plaît*, let's not get carried away. . . ."

epilogue

Two months after the Dance of the Delightfully Dead, a DeadEx arrived for Cy Clops. By this time, even Rochelle, Robecca, and Venus had all but given up on finding out who or what was behind the great monster whisper. Life as they knew it was back to normal. Until they opened the DeadEx, that is. . . .

They will come back to Monster High, as they have here. You must be vigilant in your watch.

— Signore Vitriola

And just like that, everything changed again. They might have won the battle, but the war was clearly not over. Now, if only they knew who they were fighting . . .

SCHOOL OF FEAR

Sharpen your pencils and put on a brave face.
The School of Fear is waiting for YOU!
Will you banish your fears and graduate on time?

IT'S NEVER TOO LATE TO APPLY!

www.atombooks.net

MONSTER HIGH™

FITTING IN... IS SO OUT!

MONSTER HIGH™ GHOULS RULE

The First Freaky DVD!

AVAILABLE AT ALL GOOD RETAILERS FROM 1ST OCTOBER